Miming in French

by ~~Sheila McGrory-Klyza~~

Sheila McGrory-Klyza

for Louise —
Amitiés
7/11/15

Miming in French

by Sheila McGrory-Klyza

Published by **RED 🏠 BARN BOOKS** of vermont
Shelburne, Vermont 05482

Miming in French
Copyright © 2014 by Sheila McGrory-Klyza
ISBN: 978-1-935922-77-3
Library of Congress: 2015938560
Cover design/art by Greg Forber
All rights reserved.

Published by Red Barn Books of Vermont, an imprint of the Voices of Vermonters Publishing Group, Inc.
PO Box 595
Shelburne, Vermont 05482
www.windridgebooksofvt.com

For Isabel and Faye

Chapter 1

The mountain floated in the distance, a gigantic, gray rock with sharp peaks. It made even the sky look small. Livvie squinted out the taxi window at the summit's jagged edge, outlined against electric blue. Maybe the sky was smaller here. And the sun more scorching.

"Do you see it?" Mom grabbed Livvie's arm and pointed toward the mountain. "That's Sainte Victoire. Isn't it beautiful?"

Livvie looked away, her eyes tired from the glare. Just outside the window, land blurred past, brittle and parched. "Why is everything so brown?"

"Provence is dry, especially in August. Isn't that Mediterranean light magnificent though?" Mom leaned back against the seat, beaming.

Magnificent was not what Livvie would call it. She wanted to crawl under one of those rocks out there, except then she'd probably come face to face with a lizard or a snake. Or even worse, a scorpion. The guidebook Mom forced her to read on the plane said there were scorpions in Provence, and those gray bushes outside her window looked infested with them.

And what was with the trees? Skinny and contorted, they looked nothing like trees back in Vermont. Where were the fields of lavender Mom described? And all those quaint, little villages she had raved about?

The taxi driver suddenly said something, but Livvie didn't understand a word. Mom got all excited and sputtered back to him in French. She sounded strange. Like a little kid.

"He said dinosaurs used to live here, Liv! Archeologists have found fossils over by Sainte Victoire."

"Great," Livvie muttered. "How exciting."

Mom leaned forward toward the driver and said something. His eyes smiled at Livvie in the rearview mirror, but she turned away, looking out at the bleached countryside. At least she should be thankful they had made it to France in the first place. Livvie had never flown across the ocean before, and on the flight over she kept picturing their plane exploding in midair from some crazy terrorist, with her and Mom plunging down into a swarm of sharks below.

The landscape soon gave way to buildings, to the city that would be Livvie's new home. But as the taxi slowed down with the traffic, this didn't look any better. The buildings were ancient and made out of crumbly, yellow stone. They towered over crowded, narrow sidewalks. Every now and then, crammed between the old buildings were modern ones that had the same run-down look, only newer. Even worse, they were all covered in graffiti. Red, black, and blue paint scarred the walls and doorways in an unfamiliar language.

"Why is there graffiti everywhere?" Livvie asked.

Disappointment flickered in Mom's eyes. But she forced a smile and said, "I guess it adds some character to the town. Aix-en-Provence isn't a museum town like some of those exclusive villages in the Luberon."

Livvie had no idea where the Luberon was and she didn't care. She had bigger things to worry about. Like the fact that she would be starting school in this place in just a couple weeks. Wasn't it bad enough that Mom had divorced Dad? That she had moved Livvie out of her old house and ripped her out of her school. Away from all her friends. Away from Clover. Clover was her cat. Why did she have to leave him too?

"Oh, look! It's Cours Mirabeau. This is the center of town. Kind of like their Main Street. Don't you love all the little cafés?" Mom's face was practically pressed up against the window. "And the fountains—aren't they charming?"

"It's thrilling."

"Can't you try to appreciate it, Olivia? You're so lucky at your age to be having this kind of experience."

"Yeah, I'm so lucky."

Livvie clenched her teeth and stared out at the people streaming by on the sidewalk. French people. She had nothing in common with any of them. And even if she did, she wouldn't be able to talk to them.

The taxi came to a stop in the middle of the street as another car pulled out into the traffic. In the blur of people outside Livvie's window, something flashed. Something silver. She looked closer. The crowd scattered, except for a man standing there. His face and neck were painted silver and so were his hands. Even his hair was silver. The rest of his skin was covered by a white shirt, white pants, and white sneakers. In front of him on the ground lay a small, metal bowl. He stood there by a white box not moving, his hand up by his cheek and his head cocked as if he was in the middle of a conversation. But he didn't appear to be saying a word.

The taxi driver leaned on his horn and grumbled something. But Livvie hoped they would stay stuck there for a few more minutes so she could see what this silver guy did next. Suddenly he changed position. He turned his back and did something with his hands, but Livvie couldn't tell what he was doing. The group of people clustered in front of him smiled and applauded. A few dropped some money in his bowl. One of them was a girl about Livvie's age. She had long, black, wavy hair, and her dark eyes watched the silver guy closely. Beside her stood a woman with some kind of a scarf draped around her head. It covered her hair so that only her face showed. The woman said something to the girl and turned away from the man. She walked toward the entrance of a store and motioned for the girl to follow. But the girl kept watching.

The taxi started to move again. As they drove away, Livvie turned around in her seat for one last look at the man. A crowd had circled around him, but she could still see his hands. He held them up over his head and they shimmered in the sunlight, like two silver birds. Beneath them stood the girl, her eyes raised and focused on his hands, fluttering in a delicate dance.

Then Mom was tugging on Livvie's arm again. "Livvie, that's St. John of Malta Chapel! Knights used to go there. The history here is incredible."

"Like I care."

Mom sighed and took out a lipstick. Since when did she wear lipstick?

"We're almost at the apartment, Liv. We should freshen up. You want to use my brush?"

Livvie waved it away. What she'd rather do was go back and watch that silver guy. Or maybe lean her head on Mom's shoulder, like she used to do when she was little. But Mom was busy applying her lipstick.

In a few minutes they pulled up in front of one of the graffiti-covered buildings. There was even graffiti on the front door. A stupid-looking smiley face.

"Number 12. This is it," Mom said.

Livvie climbed out of the taxi, stiff from all the travel. A taxi, a bus, two planes, the TGV train, and finally this taxi. They were all that separated this place from back home. She looked up at the three-story building made out of the same crumbly, yellow stone, like everything else. At least the blue shutters brightened it up, although they could have used a paint job.

"Grab your luggage, Liv," Mom said as she paid the taxi driver. "Our apartment's on the third floor so we might need to make a few trips."

She rang the bell while Livvie glanced up and down the street. All the buildings looked pretty much like this one, except some of them had shops on the bottom floor. Not nice shops though. The one a few doors down on the corner had a bunch of motorcycles lined up in front. Another had big photos of women with bizarre hairstyles in the window. And the place beside that had a flashing pizza sign. At least "pizza" was one word she recognized. This neighborhood couldn't be more different from where she lived back in Vermont, where their house was surrounded by fields of high grass and green forests. They had about twenty acres and their own little pond. Sometimes no one drove down their dirt road for a whole day.

The door creaked open and a man was standing there. He was tall and skinny, around Dad's age, with a head full of brown curls. He stared at them like they were at the wrong place.

"Monsieur Cantini?" Mom asked.

"Oui." He nodded.

"Je suis Diane Renner."

He looked at her blankly, and she sputtered again in French. His brow furrowed and smoothed as he nodded and said, "Oui, oui, oui, Madame." He opened the door wider, waving her in. Mom stepped into the entrance hall, lugging her bags behind her. The man rattled off something and Mom laughed. Then she turned back toward Livvie in the doorway and motioned for her to step inside. Livvie hesitated, recognizing her name in the middle of a bunch of French words pouring out of Mom's mouth. She must have introduced Livvie because the man grabbed her hand and gave it a single, firm shake. Like they had just made a deal.

"This is Monsieur Cantini," Mom said. "He owns the building. And he lives right here, on this floor."

Livvie peered past the man down the hallway. At the end, a door was open and some kind of classical music streamed out. He rattled off in French again and went through the door.

"He's getting our keys. He seems like a nice man, doesn't he?" Mom said.

"How would I know. I can't understand anything he says. Why didn't he know who we were?"

"I think he was involved with his practicing and forgot we were coming this afternoon. He's a violinist."

Monsieur Cantini reappeared with the keys and helped them carry their luggage up the stairs. As they passed the second floor landing, he jabbered in French again and Mom translated: "An older couple, the Durands, live in this apartment. They can be a little particular so if your shoes are dirty, take them off as you go up the stairs. Or you can sweep off the stairs if you prefer." Monsieur Cantini pointed to a little broom and dustpan beside their door.

How odd. They had to take their shoes off even before they went into the apartment?

They wound the rest of the way up to the third floor, as the air became progressively warmer. When they reached the top, Monsieur Cantini opened the door to the apartment, saying, "Voilà!" A clump of brown curls fell onto his forehead.

They stepped past him into a small foyer. It was painted bright white, and the floor was made out of those same reddish brown tiles. Several doors opened off the foyer, and Monsieur Cantini proceeded to lead Mom through one of the doors explaining something in French. Livvie's T-shirt was sticking to her in the heat, so she dropped her luggage and wandered into a bedroom. Two twin beds covered in red floral bedspreads dominated the space. She sat down on one of them and looked around. The room was painted a mustardy yellow, with high ceilings. Two windows went practically from the ceiling to the floor on one wall and looked like two sets of double doors made of long, narrow panels of glass. By now Livvie was covered in sweat, so she went over to let in some air.

She pushed back the long, white curtains, lifted the latch, and pulled the panels in. A breeze blew against her face as a wave of exhaustion fell over her from the two days of travel. On the other side of the window was a narrow balcony. It overlooked a little fenced-in garden that appeared to be off the back of Monsieur Cantini's apartment. Beyond the garden was a parking lot, then some more buildings, then trees. Farther out, more buildings, and those dry, brown hills. Finally, in the distance was that mountain. Saint Something. The top looked so hard and jagged, like a saw. It must be impossible to climb. Completely different from the mountains in Vermont that Livvie used to hike with Dad. Their rolling, green outline was gentle and comforting, like a cradle. When she looked out her bedroom window back home, she was surrounded by them.

And what was that thing way up on the highest peak? It looked like some kind of a cross. What was a cross doing up there? All around it the bright blue sky spread like a void. Empty of clouds. Empty of birds. Empty of everything.

"Wonderful! You found your room!" Mom burst in, startling Livvie. "Isn't it adorable? And can you believe the view?"

"No," Livvie mumbled. "I can't."

Chapter 2

After a quick tour around the apartment, Mom said, "Let's go back down to Cours Mirabeau for a bite to eat. We haven't had a real meal since dinner last night at the airport."

Even though Livvie was exhausted, she was glad to get out of the apartment, plus she might get to see that silver guy again. Outside on the sidewalk they hadn't gone ten steps before Mom grabbed Livvie's arm and shouted, "Look out!" In front of them was a pile of dog poop.

"Gross," Livvie said, stepping around it. After about ten steps there was some more. "Why are the sidewalks covered in dog poop?" Livvie asked.

"The French love their dogs," Mom said with a forced laugh. "There isn't much grass in these old cities, except for the parks, so dogs just go on the sidewalks here."

"But why don't they pick up after them?"

"They hose the sidewalks every few days, but I suppose they can't keep on top of it."

No wonder those people who lived below them were particular about clean shoes. Livvie wouldn't be wearing her flip-flops much around here.

They crossed the wide road, dodging cars, and took a narrow side street heading toward the center of town. The street was so narrow that the tops of the buildings leaned in toward each other. Cars snaked their way through. The air was cooler here in the shadow of buildings, but it was heavy with exhaust. Livvie followed Mom as she made her way down the tiny sidewalk, careful not to step in any poop.

"Oh, look! There's one of those shrines people built to ward off the plague back in Medieval times." Mom stopped and pointed up at a little alcove on the corner of a building.

Livvie peered up at the small statue perched in the alcove. It looked like something she had seen before in a church. Like Mary or some saint. Except here it was attached to a random house. A few feet beyond, strung between two windows, laundry hung from a rope. She was about to ask Mom what the laundry was doing up there beside the statue when something thundered behind them. Before she knew what was happening, a motorcycle whizzed by on the sidewalk between them and the building. Livvie shrieked, reaching for Mom.

"I forgot about those motorcycles!" Mom said. "Brilliant solution to the traffic, except for us poor pedestrians."

They resumed their walking, more cautiously now, until the maze of narrow streets finally opened up onto a square lined with cafés and official-looking buildings. Mom checked her map and said they were somewhere called Place des Prêcheurs.

"Place de what?" Livvie asked.

Mom repeated the name, and it slid off her tongue like melting butter. Even those guttural French r's. Livvie tried to repeat the words and ended up practically gagging.

"Don't worry, it'll come," Mom laughed. "We're almost there."

They stepped through an opening between two of the buildings and went down a few steps into a dim passageway. At the end of it, a small doorway opened onto Cours Mirabeau. After the dimness of the passageway, the sunlight bounced off the yellow stone buildings lining the broad street. As Livvie stood there, blinking in the sun, Mom looked up and down the sidewalk. This one was much wider than those others.

"Let's go this way," Mom said, turning right toward a string of busy cafés.

She chose a place called Les Deux Garçons and they took a table by the edge of the sidewalk. A half a block away, the silver guy's white box sat in the shade of a tree. But he was nowhere to be seen, and neither was the girl with the dark hair who had been watching him.

"Don't you love this?" Mom said. "The café life."

"It reminds me of Burlington. All the little restaurants on Church Street."

"Yeah, but this is the real thing. The US copied the idea from the French."

"I don't see why that makes it any better here. I'd much rather be sitting at Sweetwaters right now. At least there I could read the menu."

"Come on, Liv. Let's not be negative. Wait until you taste the food here. Even simple food tastes fabulous."

Mom ordered for them—a salad with goat cheese for her, an omelet for Livvie. When the food came, Livvie wasn't hungry so she just picked at her omelet while Mom went on and on about all the things Livvie was going to love about France. People streamed past their table looking happy and relaxed. Like they belonged here. Except for the groups of tourists who were easy to spot with their maps and sun hats. They looked out of place too, but at least they had somewhere to go back home to.

Livvie kept looking down at the white box on the sidewalk, hoping the silver guy would come back. Where could he be? She was beginning to wonder if maybe she mixed up the location when he walked up to the box and sat down. He put one elbow on his knee. Then he leaned forward and put his chin on the back of his hand. The pose looked familiar.

"Mom, what's that guy over there doing?"

"He looks like a street performer. Some kind of mime."

"What's a mime?"

"They communicate using gestures, without speaking at all. Kind of like acting, but not using any words. I would find it incredibly frustrating, wouldn't you?"

Livvie shrugged. "What pose is he doing?"

"It looks like The Thinker. That sculpture by Rodin." Mom sopped up some dressing with a piece of bread. "We'll have to go see it sometime in Paris. Pretty clever for a street performer."

The mime held his Thinker pose for a few minutes while a small crowd gathered around him. As the crowd grew, Livvie couldn't see him anymore, except for an occasional flash of silver or white between gaps in the audience. Finally the crowd applauded and he climbed up on top of his box. Now he was visible from the shoulders up.

He put his hands above his head and pressed against something. A ceiling? He looked surprised and pressed again. Then he brought his arms out to each side and did the same thing. And then out in front like he was pressing against a wall. He knocked on it with a panicked look on his face. He knocked all around himself like he was trapped inside something. A box? He pounded the air above his head and out in front of him, his face growing more and more desperate.

"That's a good idea for tonight, don't you think, Liv?" Mom's question pulled Livvie away.

"Huh?"

"For tonight. For dinner."

"Um, sure." Livvie didn't bother to ask what she had said.

While Mom paid the bill, Livvie stole glances at the mime. He had stopped pounding and was jiggling something in front of him. Maybe a door. A way out. He finally pushed it open and relief spread across his face. The audience broke into applause. Then the mime hopped down from his box and disappeared into the crowd.

Later that night, Livvie lay in bed listening to the street sounds outside. Car motors, someone calling out in French, some kind of strange siren. They were so different from the sounds outside her bedroom back home. Sounds of crickets and birds. All kinds of birds, depending on the time of year. Bluebirds, black-capped chickadees, robins. Sometimes even an owl. The room was brighter here too, from the lights in the parking lot out back. And the bed was harder. She tossed around trying to get comfortable, but her stomach was making a fist.

Only a couple months before, Livvie was a normal, eleven-year-old girl living with her mom and dad and cat in Hinesburg, Vermont. She had lived in the same house all her life and gone to the same school. All she could hope was that any day now Mom would come to her senses and they would go back home. This would just be some kind of bizarre vacation. They would unpack their dirty clothes, open all the windows, and she would flop down on her bed, like when they would get back from the beach every summer. But someone else was living in their house now, and Dad was living in Boston, and she and Mom were all the way across the ocean. Her old life had simply disappeared.

Tears squeezed out the corners of Livvie's eyes. Why did Mom have to make Dad leave? Why couldn't she have let him try harder, like she always said to Livvie when she wasn't giving her all to something? Why couldn't Mom have tried harder?

After Dad left, Livvie had spent a couple afternoons with him, but he had never talked about his plans. When he came and packed up his things, Mom had taken her to Montreal for the weekend. She talked with him a few times on the phone after that, and he asked her about softball, and the lake, little things. It just seemed like he was away on a long trip, not that he had moved to another state. Except each time at the end of the call he had said, "I love you, Livvie. You know I love you, don't you?" He had never asked her that question before.

Livvie's stomach clenched tighter and tears burned her cheeks, so she tried to think of something different. Her thoughts jumped to the street mime, standing in the middle of a crowd, but separate from everyone else. She pictured him knocking and pounding on the walls of his imaginary box. The desperate look in his eyes. How had he ended up in Aix? Had he moved from somewhere else too or had he been born here? And why had he chosen to be a mime out of all the other possible things a person could do? She wondered how he came up with his ideas and if he practiced. Or if he did whatever popped into his head. Was it hard not to talk with anyone all day? Maybe that was what he liked about it. But what did he do when he got lonely? Suddenly she thought of the girl with black, wavy hair who was watching the mime. How the mime's hands, like silver birds, danced above the girl. And how the girl looked as if she wanted to reach up and catch one of the birds. Or maybe hold onto it and fly up into the sky. Livvie fell asleep imagining herself holding onto one of those birds too, flying.

Chapter 3

"Don't forget to sit up straight in your chair—the French don't like slouching—and try to use some of your French," Mom said as she tied a silk scarf around her neck.

"What French?" Livvie asked. "I don't speak any French."

"You know, bonjour and merci—use a few words like that. It'll impress the directrice."

"Yeah, and then she'll think I can speak the language and will go on and on in French and I won't understand anything she's saying!"

"I can never get these to look right. How do those French women do it?" Mom sighed and retied her scarf. "We'd better get going, though. We don't want to be late. The directrice said there would be someone waiting to let us in."

"How am I supposed to learn anything at school if I don't speak the language? Those dialogues you made me listen to were worthless."

"You're a smart girl. You'll learn quickly." Mom slicked on some lipstick. "You're fortunate to be able to be immersed at a young age. I slogged through six years of French before coming here in college and it wasn't until then that I learned to speak it."

"Right, Mom, I know. What's a directrice anyway?"

"The school principal. Her name's Madame Moreau, but we should use her formal title, Madame la Directrice."

"That's what she's called? She sounds like some kind of queen. I can't even pronounce it."

Livvie practiced saying the principal's title as they walked over to the school. It was around the corner from their apartment in a big building made of that same crumbly, yellow stone. Someone had spray-painted over the graffiti in yellow though so the facade looked all blotchy. Like a person's face after she's been crying. The building was u-shaped and in the center was a paved courtyard separated from the sidewalk by a tall, iron fence. A woman was waiting at the gate to let them in. She had a key and promptly locked the gate again behind them. So far this was more like a prison than a school. What would have happened if they had been late?

"Where's all the playground equipment?" Livvie whispered to Mom. There were no swings or monkey bars, and not even a basketball hoop in sight.

"That's an American thing. They don't have those at school here."

Livvie's heart raced as they walked across the courtyard. What would she do at recess? If there were swings like back home, she could at least go swing on them and look like she was doing it by choice. Here, there would be nowhere to hide.

Madame la Directrice stood up from behind her desk to greet them even before they reached her door. "Bonjour, Madame Renner. Bonjour, Olivia," she said, extending her hand to each of them, giving an efficient shake.

Livvie tried her best to pronounce her title correctly, but Madame la Directrice winced behind her red-lipped smile. They all sat down, Madame la Directrice behind her large desk and Livvie and Mom in two hard wooden chairs positioned side by side facing her. She then launched into a torrent of French, all the while shuffling through papers and swiveling around several times to a file cabinet immediately behind her.

Mom stared at her, adjusting her scarf and nodding vacantly. Finally, there was a pause in the flood of words and Madame la Directrice looked at Mom expectantly. When Mom didn't answer, Madame la Directrice said, "My English, it not very good," unapologetically. Mom stammered something back in French, and Madame la Directrice resumed her monologue. Livvie sat up straight in her chair and let Mom try to do the talking.

Livvie would have been in sixth grade back home, but since she didn't speak French she was going to be in the equivalent of 5th grade here. To make it easier, Mom said. They called it CM2. Madame la Directrice's shiny, red lips kept repeating the name Monsieur Simon, so Livvie guessed he was her teacher. Other than that, it all sounded like some strange birdsong. Madame la Directrice's short hair hugged her head like a dark cap, a dark cap that was constantly in motion. As Livvie watched it darting around above the desk, a lump formed in her throat. How could she possibly do any work at this school? Back home she had gotten mostly A's, but here she would be lucky if she could even write a sentence! Why was Mom making her do this? It was so unfair that she had dragged Livvie across the ocean and completely changed her life so she could live out some dream of becoming a chic Frenchwoman.

The lump was getting bigger, but the last thing Livvie wanted to do was burst into tears in front of Madame la Directrice. So she willed her mind to think of something else, something happy. The trouble was that everything that made her happy—like Dad, Clover, her best friend Annabel, ice skating on her pond—was a million miles away.

Just when the lump was about to explode, Madame la Directrice stood up again and leaned over to shake Mom's hand. Mom still had that vacant look on her face. But she flashed a smile and said in a tight voice, "Merci beaucoup, Madame."

Madame la Directrice gave Mom a packet of papers and turned to Livvie with her hand outstretched. Livvie stood up and shook it, but didn't say a word.

After they had been led back out across the courtyard and through the gate, Mom said, "That wasn't so bad. Except she spoke faster than is humanly possible. I caught about every third word. What did you think?"

The lump was getting smaller now that they had left, and part of Livvie wanted to tell Mom how she had felt in there. But another part of her didn't want to tell her anything, so she said, "My teacher's name is Monsieur Simon. That's the only thing I could understand."

"It's great you could follow what she was saying, Livvie. I knew you'd pick it up quickly. But it's pronounced missyew," Mom said. "You don't really pronounce the r."

"Missyew," Livvie repeated, but she stressed the wrong syllable, the first one, so it sounded like she was saying "miss you."

"Close enough. The directrice gave me a list of materials you need for the first day." Mom slid a sheet of paper out of the packet. It was a long list, with about thirty items on it. "I have no idea what any of this is. Except stylo, which means pen. I guess we'll have to look the rest of these up in the dictionary. That'll take some time."

A motorcycle roared past them and Livvie shouted over the noise, "Thirty words? You think that'll take time? I'll need to read the dictionary all day long!"

"Livvie, calm down. It'll be fine. It might be difficult at first, but you'll learn French quickly. You'll wake up one morning and everything will click. It's the best way to learn a language."

Livvie looked at the ground, watching out for dog poop, until they reached their street, Cours Saint Louis. She tried to say the street name in her head the French way, kor sang lewee, not like the city in Missouri, but it didn't sound right. Why was everything in Aix named after saints? And what kind of city was named Aix? Aix was short for Aix-en-Provence, but most people just called the city Aix, which sounded like the letter x. Even weirder, although their apartment was on the third floor, for some reason it was called the second floor in France. The bottom floor was called the rez-de-chaussée, or floor 0. Livvie was glad they didn't live on floor 0. Floor 0 in the city of x would have been a pretty sorry address.

When they got to their building, Mom dug around in her purse for the key. Livvie looked up at the graffiti face, at its sneering smile. As they stepped inside, Mom reminded Livvie to take off her sandals. She thought about refusing, but the last thing she wanted was those old people yelling at her for getting dirt on the stairs so she slid them off. Passing the old couple's apartment, Livvie heard muffled voices inside. For some reason she hadn't met them yet. Mom kept saying she was going to knock on their door to introduce herself, but so far she hadn't. The sound of a violin whined out of Monsieur Cantini's apartment as they climbed up the rest of the stairs.

As they entered the apartment, the colors all jumped out at Livvie. They were so bright and gaudy, so unfamiliar. The painted furniture. The floral fabrics. The tile floor. Those tall windows that opened in.

Back in Vermont their house wasn't huge or fancy, but it was comfortable and cozy. The floors were either wooden or carpeted, and the walls were painted in soft colors like tan or beige. Her bedroom was a pale blue and she had a big, comfy bed. Since they lived out in the country, they were surrounded by wide, open space. Everything was bigger back home. The furniture, the bathroom, the refrigerator. In France, everything was small and crowded, as if the country was inhabited by a tribe of miniature people.

Livvie went into the kitchen to get a glass of water and stepped out on the balcony. Sitting down on one of the chairs, she stared over the tiled rooftops at the mountain, at its hulking, gray outline. She tried to imagine she was back at home on their deck. Dad had on his silly chef's apron and was grilling some steaks. Mom was in the garden gathering tomatoes for a salad.

This exact scene happened only a year ago. Why did Dad leave Vermont and move to Boston? He didn't even like cities. And he had loved his job at the radio station, at least most of the time. He had lots of friends there, like Toby and Jill. And that new DJ Becky, who stopped by the house one day on her bike. Dad had gotten her some iced tea and she had helped Livvie lure Clover out from under the deck.

Dad would hate it here in France. How small and crowded everything was. He was tall and broad—not fat, but big like a lot of American men were. He gave giant bear hugs and sometimes would still give Livvie a piggyback ride. She loved how patient he was when he was coaching her softball team. She loved leaning against him on the couch with Clover stretched out over both of their laps while they watched a movie. She loved how he called her

Livbug, and how he would laugh at something goofy Mom did and then give her a kiss on the forehead. But now Dad had Clover and Mom had her. She wondered if they actually talked about the two of them in the same conversation.

Livvie stared and stared at Sainte Victoire, willing its sharp edges to soften and turn green, but they didn't. "Everything will be better in France, you'll see," Mom had said before they left. "Even my name sounds better. I've never liked my name, but in French Diane sounds almost beautiful. Dee-ahnnnn-nn." When she dragged out the n, she raised her arm in a dramatic way like she was singing opera.

Mom was wrong. Everything wasn't better in France. It was much, much worse. Diane might sound better in French, but Olivia didn't. Oh-leev-ee-ah was bad enough, but Livvie was pronounced Lee-vee. Half the time she didn't know if people were trying to talk to her, or if they were saying something about leaving.

Chapter 4

Over croissants with jam the next morning, Mom said she had translated Madame la Directrice's list and later that morning they would go shopping for school supplies.

"I can't wait," Livvie muttered.

"Come on, it'll be fun to see how they're different from what you used back in the States."

"But I was gonna get on the computer. I wanted to chat with Annabel."

"She won't be up yet. Remember the six hour time difference? That can wait 'til later."

On the walk over to Cours Mirabeau, Livvie dragged her feet. She had been looking forward to chatting with Annabel and finding out what was going on back home. The time difference made it hard. Then she remembered she would get to see the mime. He was usually there every day in front of the same café. He was always in a different pose, sometimes sitting, sometimes standing. But always wearing the same white clothing and silver paint on his skin. Like some sort of magical being.

As they turned down Cours Mirabeau, there he was, surrounded by a small group. He looked shorter for some reason. Then Livvie saw his knees were slightly bent like he was cowering from something. His arms were tucked up by his chest and his eyes were round as an owl's. He lifted one arm up in front of his face and peeked out over top, still cowering. Suddenly he crouched behind his box, trying to hide. Trying to get as small as he could. What was he hiding from?

Livvie slowed down in front of him, but Mom took her arm and pulled her past. "Come on, Liv. We have a lot to do this morning."

"But I wanted to watch," Livvie said, looking back at the mime, at his silver head peering up over his box. What was he afraid of?

"Watch where you're going! You almost ran into that lady."

"Sorry," Livvie mumbled.

Mom pushed her sunglasses up on her head and led Livvie through the electronic, sliding doors of Monoprix. The fluorescent lighting and muzak of old American songs jolted her back to the organized world of a superstore. They stepped on the escalator and Mom consulted the list. "Some of this doesn't make much sense, but we'll do our best. Let's see, one blue ink pen. Easy enough."

On the first floor were several aisles of school supplies, so they picked a less crowded one. The aisle was still crammed with people—parents pulling things off shelves, kids staring up at the choices, teenagers standing around in groups. It looked as if everyone in town had had the same idea. The aisle they chose didn't have any pens. Instead it was lined with notebooks and folders in all shapes and sizes, so they walked around to the next one.

"What do you think they mean by ink pen?" Mom asked. "Here's a ball point and a roller ball. And here's a fine point marker and a medium point one."

"I have no idea. Do you think it really matters? I mostly use pencil for my work at home."

"Yeah, they aren't very specific about it. Why don't you just pick one."

Livvie opted for the roller ball, and they moved on to the next item on the list, a notebook. There were countless choices, but the list specified it had to be 21 by 30 centimeters. Livvie had forgotten how everything was in metrics here—yet another thing to have to learn.

They found the correct sized notebook and continued on down the list, collecting pencils, an eraser, a sharpener, markers, colored pencils, and an ominously thick dictionary. Livvie flipped through it but it was all in French, so it wouldn't do her much good.

"We're almost to the bottom of the list," Mom said. "The next thing is a binder. Why don't you grab one of those and I'll go get a ruler."

Livvie went back to the aisle where she remembered seeing binders and wound through the crowd. When she got to the shelves stacked high with options in different colors, a girl about her age was standing in front of them looking up at all the choices. Her dark, wavy hair was pulled back in a ponytail.

The girl glanced at Livvie and reached up to pull a purple binder off the shelf. As she opened it up, a woman came around the corner talking to her in French. The girl said something back, and the woman looked down at the sheet of paper in her hands. She had a dark green scarf wrapped around her head, covering everything but her face. Like that woman Livvie had seen the first day by the mime. Maybe this was the same woman. And the same girl. She was shopping for school supplies too. Maybe she went to the same school. She could be in the same grade. Maybe she even knew the mime.

Livvie realized she was staring at them when the woman looked up and their eyes met. The woman frowned and quickly looked away. She said something to the girl, who glanced at Livvie again. Then the girl gathered up her things and followed the woman out of the aisle. Livvie stood there looking after them. Like someone watching a car long after it's pulled out of a driveway.

"There you are." Mom came around the corner lugging the overflowing shopping basket. "Did you pick out a binder?"

Livvie grabbed a purple one like the girl had chosen.

"Purple? I didn't think you like purple."

"It's okay."

"Fine, it's up to you." Mom looked down at the list. "The last thing is une grande chemise. I think it's some kind of an art smock."

"An art smock? I haven't used one of those since kindergarten. What kind of school is this?"

Mom didn't answer, but Livvie would find out soon enough. School started in two days.

Chapter 5

"Mom, where's my jeans skirt?" Livvie called out as she dug around in her dresser drawer.

"It's on the drying rack. I thought you got everything ready for school last night. We don't have time for trying on five different outfits this morning. That metal gate swings closed at 8:30 and if you're not at school by then, tant pis!"

"I did get everything ready," Livvie said under her breath.

It was true. But in the morning, the outfit she had picked out wasn't right. Nothing was right. She hadn't gotten much sleep and, as she spun the drying rack around to look for her skirt, her hands trembled. Livvie hated the drying rack, but at least it was better than hanging their laundry out the window. She found her skirt. It was dry, but stiff as cardboard, so she bunched it up into a ball to soften it and slid it on.

"C'mon, Liv. You need to eat something before school," Mom called from the kitchen.

Livvie's stomach was in knots, but she sat down at the table and took a few bites of buttered toast.

"You'll have a nice, big meal at lunch—school lunches here are so much better than back in the US—but it's important to start the first day off with a good breakfast."

Mom was chattering away in that fake cheerful way Livvie recognized. It was her first official day at work, so she was probably nervous too. But she had already met a lot of the people there and most of them spoke English. Plus she was doing her same job at the same computer company, just in a different office, so what was the big deal? Livvie was going off to a completely new school full of total strangers speaking what might as well be Swahili. Her hands shook as she forced down one last bite of toast. Then she grabbed her backpack full of supplies and they headed down the stairs.

It was only a three-minute walk to school, but Livvie struggled to keep up with Mom. As they rounded the corner by the motorcycle shop, she could see a large crowd gathering by the front gate. Young children in colorful, new clothes held their parents' hands. Older kids around Livvie's age smiled and kissed each other on both cheeks. Even the boys.

They were soon swept up into the crowd and voices sang out around them. Everyone was speaking the language of the first day of school. Images flooded into Livvie's head. Her first grade teacher Mrs. McCoy and the way she smelled of roses and crayons. The annual opening assembly in the gym when there was always a slide show of the previous year. Walking into the new wing for the first time with Annabel last year. Laughing at lunchtime with Annabel, Sarah, and Kendall over some funny story from the summer. The lump rose in Livvie's throat again and she bit her lip hard to stop it.

"Look," Mom said, putting her arm on Livvie's shoulder. "It's la Directrice. That must be the principal for the lower grades beside her."

Two women descended the stairs on the other side of the gate. They were both dressed in short, fitted suits and wore red smiles. Madame la Directrice held up the key. With dramatic flair, she unlocked the gate and the two of them swung it open. It was all very formal compared to the first day of school back in Vermont. Madame la Directrice addressed the crowd, which shushed and leaned in to listen.

"What's she saying, Mom?"

"She's greeting everyone, and I think they're going to have the classes enter by grade. Seems like a disorganized way to do things, if you ask me, but they obviously have it all under control."

Soon the youngest children, the first graders, kissed their parents goodbye and filed through the gate. A few cried and clung to their anxious-looking adults. The next grade was called, and the next. Before Livvie knew it,

Madame la Directrice announced CM2, her grade, the highest in the school. By this time the crowd had thinned. Most of the remaining students stood together in small groups, with their parents clustered nearby. Mom squeezed Livvie's shoulder and kissed her hard on the cheek. Usually Livvie didn't like it when Mom kissed her in public, but at that moment she wanted to throw her arms around Mom like one of those first graders.

"It'll be fine, I know it will," Mom said.

And then Livvie was walking toward the gate, still biting her lip, her backpack heavy on her shoulder. She fell in line behind the other students, and they proceeded up the stairs into the courtyard. There, the CM2s all quickly scattered again into groups that laughed and talked as if they had known each other for years. They probably had, like Livvie knew all of her classmates back at Hinesburg Elementary. She edged toward one of the walls surrounding the courtyard and looked around for anyone else who was alone. A skinny boy with glasses walked toward a bench in the shade of a large tree. He took a comic book out of his backpack, sat down, and opened it.

There was a girl off by herself too. Her back was to Livvie and she stood a few feet away from a group of smiling, laughing girls. They were all really pretty and wore bright, stylish clothes. They ignored the other girl, who kept standing there. Every so often she tucked a strand of her black, wavy hair behind her ear.

A bell rang and the girl turned her head. It was the girl from Monoprix. The one Livvie had seen on the first day with the mime. She went to this school after all. But why weren't those other girls including her? Maybe she was new too.

"Alors, tout le monde!" A voice called out from the other side of the courtyard.

The voice belonged to a short, bald man standing by the entrance to the building. On either side of him were two women. He continued speaking and all the students began to fall in line in front of one of the three adults. The man had to be Monsieur Simon. Livvie followed the students streaming over to line up by him. The girl from Monoprix got in her line. So did a few of the girls from the laughing group, each with a sleek schoolbag slung crossways over her shoulder. The bags were different colors, but they all had a picture of a Scottie dog on them and the word "Chipie." Livvie's own backpack hung awkwardly, twisting her back. How had these girls managed to fit all their supplies into those slim bags?

Monsieur Simon stopped talking and led the line up the stairs to a classroom. With its green chalkboards and desks grouped in threes, it was similar to classrooms in Livvie's old school. There weren't any computers in the room, though, and everything looked older and a little drab. The colorful posters and artwork that usually hung on the walls of her classrooms back in Vermont were missing, and in their place were charts in cursive, maps, and mathematical tables. Livvie's stomach clenched as she glanced around for a place to sit.

Everyone was sliding into chairs, so she quickly chose a desk in the back near the door. A boy with short, blond hair and freckles slouched in beside her. The girl with the black hair walked up to a desk in the front and sat down by herself. If she was new, she was pretty brave to be sitting up in front. But then again, she did speak French. The three girls with the Chipie bags sat together. The one in the middle with the long, auburn hair whispered something to the other two and they both giggled.

Monsieur Simon sat down at a big desk in the front of the room. He opened up a folder and began speaking. One of the students responded. Monsieur Simon said a few more words and another student responded the same way. It seemed like a list of names, so Livvie figured Monsieur Simon must have been taking roll. Her name was toward the end so she watched what the other students did. When he called out "Olivia Renner" with his funny French pronunciation, she answered "présent" as the other students had. She tried her best to use the French r, but mustn't have pulled it off because Monsieur immediately said, "Ah, tu es l'américaine, oui?"

Livvie understood the word américaine, so she nodded and said, "Oui."

Big mistake. He jabbered something in French and she sat there feeling dumb while everyone turned around to look at her. Her cheeks burned and her heart pounded as she tried to think of what to do. But soon he was on to the next name and she was thankfully forgotten.

The rest of the morning Livvie stayed mute and tried to follow what the other students were doing. At least she could recognize numbers when Monsieur wrote them on the board, but she had no idea what she was supposed to do with them. When he handed out a sheet of paper with a few paragraphs in French on it, she stared at the black ink until the letters danced and blurred to gray. Everybody else opened their notebooks and started writing. Livvie opened hers and doodled in a corner of the page.

Monsieur circled the room and when he passed her desk, he stopped. "You not speak French, Olivia?" he asked, squatting down beside her desk.

"No, not much."

"In three month you will, vraiment. I help you with French and you help me with English, d'accord? During English lesson, which begin later in year, you be helper, yes?"

Livvie nodded and he gave her a pat on the arm.

"Paul, you speak a little English, n'est-ce pas?" Monsieur Simon said to the boy next to her.

The boy glanced up from his notebook. He hadn't written much. "Yes, my father's English."

"Bon, you explain what to do to Olivia, d'accord?"

"Oui, Monsieur," Paul mumbled.

After that, Paul slid his notebook over every once in a while so Livvie could see what he had written. It wasn't much help since it was all in French. A few times he leaned over and whispered something about an assignment. But mostly he didn't seem especially happy to have been given the additional work of helping her.

Livvie made the mistake of sitting beside Paul at lunch. Why had she thought he would make an effort to translate if he didn't have to? He completely ignored her and spoke in French with the other boys at the table. They ignored her too, except to smile at the way she held her knife and fork. Livvie knew the French held them in the opposite hands with the fork pointed down, which made eating look more proper. But she was determined to eat the American way, even if it did look like she was holding her fork like a shovel.

The whole lunch was much more proper than back home. The tables were covered in white cloths, and stern-faced women walked around serving the food in courses. They placed large platters in the middle of the tables, and the students served themselves. It was all so strange for a school cafeteria, but Livvie had to admit that it beat those red plastic trays with compartments for all the little blobs of food.

Suddenly Paul and his friends burst out in laughter. Livvie looked away and scanned the room. She wished she had sat with the other new girl, the girl with the dark hair, who was at a table with kids who weren't talking to her either. She was just sitting there quietly eating her meal like Livvie was. The girl knew exactly where to go and how everything at the school worked, though, which was odd for a new student. But maybe all French schools were pretty much the same.

The other new girl didn't look very different from a lot of the other students at the school. Many of them had dark hair and eyes. Although her skin was a little darker. With Livvie's lighter hair and blue eyes, she was more unusual. That's not at all how it was in Vermont. Her school had had a few Asian and black kids, but mostly everyone was pretty fair. Something else about the girl was different from the other students, but Livvie couldn't figure out what. Her name was a little unusual. Malika. But a lot of French names sounded different to Livvie. Maybe it was her clothes, which were pretty basic. Tan pants and a light blue cotton blouse. They weren't nearly as bright and fashionable as the clothes that the group with the matching Chipie bags was wearing.

Those three girls were sitting together, which was no surprise. A few girls from the other classes were sitting with them too. They all had the same stylish, confident look. So happy and perfect, like they had stepped out of a catalogue. They smiled and chattered while they ate their lunch like they were at a party.

Livvie watched them as she nibbled at her chicken and potatoes. It tasted pretty good for cafeteria food, but she wasn't hungry. At one point, the girl with the auburn hair looked over at Livvie and said something to the others. Her thick, arching eyebrows moved up and down over her gray eyes as she spoke. Livvie looked at her plate and chased a pea around with her fork. She couldn't scoop it up so she squished it. The loud voices of Paul, Peahead Paul, and his friends echoed in her ears.

At last, the bell rang. Livvie followed the other students out to the courtyard to what looked like recess. She stepped out into the glaring sunshine while everybody scattered into their groups again. If only there was a swing set. Then she wouldn't be so out of place with nothing to do and no one to talk to. She found a shady spot along the wall away from everybody. Leaning back against the cool stone, she closed her eyes. The courtyard and all the CM2s disappeared. She imagined herself flying away, back across the ocean to Vermont. Like the black-tailed gull that had flown all the way from Japan to Lake Champlain the year before. Dad was so excited and took her and Annabel over to the beach to see it through his binoculars. They had gotten bored after about five minutes and went wading in the freezing cold lake until Dad was finished. She and Annabel had tried to see who could keep their feet in the water the longest. Livvie always won.

The sound of someone shouting made Livvie open her eyes. It was one of Peahead Paul's friends jumping around with a soccer ball, or football as it was called in France. The other boys were patting him on the back. He must have made a goal or something. They were over on the other side of the courtyard, beyond the bench by the tree.

That girl Malika was sitting on the bench by herself. She just sat there, not doing anything except looking at the other kids, her soft, round face open and friendly. Livvie wished she could go over and talk to her. Maybe they could be friends since they were both new. If she was new. But why else would she be sitting all by herself if she wasn't?

Livvie followed where Malika's eyes were focused. At that group of girls again. The ones with the matching bags. They were by the other courtyard wall, across from Livvie in the sun. They were standing around in a circle talking, and every now and then their laughter floated up out of the courtyard like a bunch of colorful balloons.

Livvie closed her eyes again and thought about Annabel and Sarah and Kendall. About the 6th grade play she wouldn't be in with them. And the softball team she wouldn't be on. About the overnight trip to Ottawa she wouldn't get to go on. Finally, the bell rang and she filed back into the building behind the others.

Back in the classroom Livvie returned to her seat beside Peahead Paul, and for the rest of the afternoon she listened to Monsieur Simon spew out words that didn't make any sense. She would have closed her eyes to make them all disappear like she had at recess, but she didn't want to call any attention to herself. So she stared at the chalkboard until everything blurred into a hazy wash of green.

Chapter 6

Mom was waiting for Livvie at the gate at 4:30. "How'd it go?" she asked with too much enthusiasm.

"I don't know. I couldn't understand anything the teacher said."

"Does he speak any English?"

"A little. I sit beside a boy whose dad is English and he translated some for me."

"How nice! I knew there would be some other kids who speak English. What's his name?"

"Paul." Livvie shrugged. "And guess what. I have the wrong kind of pen. I need an ink pen, the kind with a cartridge. They use them for everything, even math. It's so weird. And I have the wrong kind of markers. I need the kind with calligraphy tips."

"No problem. Why don't we head over to Monoprix now? We can get an ice cream to celebrate your first day of French school. How does that sound?"

"I saw a sign for Ben and Jerry's at one of the cafés. Can we go there?" Livvie had been wanting to go there since she had seen the familiar cartoon cows on their first day in Aix.

"You mean that silly place called Uncle Sam's with all the American food? French ice cream is so much better. Wait 'til you try it. You won't believe how good it is."

"Sure." Why did Mom think everything French was always so much better? Livvie would much rather have had Ben & Jerry's, but it wasn't worth the effort to try to convince Mom.

"So, did you make friends with any of the girls at school?"

"Not really. It's a little hard to make friends when I don't speak the same language."

"Give it time, Liv. It's only the first day."

Yeah, the first day of a million horrible days. Livvie shifted her backpack to the other shoulder and said, "How'd your first day at work go?"

"It was great. The people are nice. There are quite a few Americans in the office."

"You're lucky."

"Actually, I'd prefer it if there weren't so many. I didn't come here to hang out with a bunch of Americans."

Mom got a call from someone on her cell phone and chattered away in French as they wound through the narrow streets to Cours Mirabeau. When they turned down toward Monoprix, Livvie looked for the mime in his usual place. There he was, standing in front of his box. A few people were clustered off to the side watching him. He had a small bouquet of purple pansies in his hand. He held them up to his nose and breathed in deeply.

Mom slipped her phone back in her purse and said, "What were we talking about, Liv?"

"I don't know." Livvie slowed down as they approached the mime. "Let's see what he does next."

The mime brought the flowers down from his nose and held them out to Mom with a smile. "Non, merci," she said, steering Livvie away by the elbow. "I won't be flattered by a bouquet of fake flowers."

Livvie glanced back over her shoulder. The mime blew a kiss to Mom's back. One of the people from the cluster stepped forward and dropped some coins in his bowl.

"Do you think he's poor, Mom?"

"Who?"

"The mime."

"Oh. Probably," Mom said as they stepped through Monoprix's door. "Why else would he be doing it? There's a big unemployment problem in

France. A lot of people can't find jobs."

"Maybe we could give him some money when we go by."

"France is generous to the poor. There are lots of programs for them, much more than in the US. Who knows what he spends his money on. It could go to drugs or alcohol, for all we know." Mom stepped onto the escalator. "Come on, let's focus on finding an ink pen."

That night as Livvie lay in bed, her stomach clenched at the idea of going back to school the next day. Earlier, she had finally gotten to chat with Annabel and heard all about 6th grade and how much everyone missed her, especially Sarah and Kendall. Livvie's eyes welled up as she thought about her friends and her old school, but she squeezed the tears back in. Mom was out on the balcony right outside her window and Livvie didn't want her to know she was crying.

So she tried to think about something else, something happy. Like Mom always used to suggest when Livvie was little and had had a nightmare. But Livvie couldn't think of anything happy that didn't make her sad. So she thought about the street mime again. How he had offered Mom the bouquet of flowers. She wondered if he made enough money to live off of. Had he lost his job and needed to resort to being a street performer? Maybe he had a family. He didn't seem like he was on drugs or anything. He was different from other street performers around town who looked like they lived on the street too. Maybe he was divorced. Did he have kids? It was hard to tell how old he was with all that silver paint on his skin. Were his kids around her age? Maybe his wife had a good job so they weren't poor. Livvie wondered what his voice sounded like.

Chapter 7

School wasn't much different the next day, or the day after that. Or the day after that. September slowly gave way to the cooler days of October. The light, though still much brighter than back in Vermont, softened, and the yellow buildings of Aix glowed golden in the late afternoon.

Livvie hardly spoke in class except to ask Peahead a question if she didn't understand what to do. Mostly she sat and watched Monsieur Simon as he scrawled verbs on the board, or math problems, or dates from French history. She tried to follow along and copy things down in her notebook, but using the ink pen had taken some getting used to. Usually she ended up with a lot of blue blotches on her paper and ink all over her fingers.

From her position in the back of the room, Livvie had a good view of the rest of the class. The Chipies—that's what she called the girls with the matching schoolbags—usually looked like eager students paying attention to Monsieur. But when he turned his back to write on the board, they whispered or passed notes. Livvie had learned their names were Nicole, Sylvie, and Pilar. But they were always together and usually wearing clothing with that Chipie dog logo, so she just thought of them as the Chipies.

Nicole, the one with the auburn hair, was the leader. The others clustered around her on the playground and vied for seats beside her at lunch. Sylvie was the shortest one and usually wore her straight, light brown hair in a high ponytail. She had a small, turned-up nose and a ready smile. Like she was aiming to be a cheerleader. If they even had cheerleaders in France. Pilar was exotic looking with her dark eyes and head full of long, black curls. She had a hard time sitting still in class and was one of the louder ones at recess. Her laughter always rang above the other girls'. They were never mean to anyone else, but it was obvious they were part of an exclusive group. At lunch and recess, they huddled together with their friends from other classes who were equally pretty and well dressed. Every so often Livvie caught them looking at her, but mostly they ignored anyone who wasn't in their circle.

Some other kids in the class had gradually gotten friendlier. But since they didn't speak much English and Livvie didn't speak French, there wasn't a lot they could talk about. So after a while they usually gave up. One boy named Thomas, who was kind of like the class clown, broke into the "Happy Birthday" song whenever he stood beside Livvie in line. It was odd, but Mom said he was probably trying to make friends and that was all the English he knew.

Lunch and recess were the hardest times of day for Livvie. The other kids were so glad to finally be free to hang out and talk to each other, but she ended up off by herself feeling stupid. At least nobody ever made fun of her. The other outsider in the class was Malika. Livvie still wasn't sure whether she was new this year or not. She kept to herself, but she was really smart. Maybe that was why she didn't fit in. Or maybe she was just shy. Every day Livvie considered sitting with her at lunch. But since Malika didn't talk with any of the other kids, why would she talk to Livvie? The idea of the two of them sitting there across from each other not saying a word was worse than sitting down with a group of kids who talked to each other as if she wasn't there.

The woman in the headscarf was often waiting for Malika by the gate after school. Before coming to France, Livvie had never seen a woman wearing a headscarf in person. Only on TV. She knew Muslim women wore them from news stories about the Middle East. Livvie figured that woman was Malika's mother, so Malika must be a Muslim too. Maybe that had something to do with why she didn't fit in. Livvie didn't remember seeing any other women with headscarves around the school gate, and not many others walking around Aix.

At recess Malika had started bringing out a book. She sat on the bench and read for the whole hour. Livvie usually stood in her shady spot by the wall. Sometimes she closed her eyes and went back home in her mind. Sometimes she watched the goings-on in the courtyard like a red-tailed hawk from its hidden perch. Except she wasn't hidden. Everybody just acted as if she was.

At least September was over and October was a short month for school because of Toussaint, the French word for All Saints. In the US, All Saints Day was merely the day after Halloween and nobody Livvie knew did anything special for it. Everyone was always tired out from trick-or-treating. People didn't trick-or-treat in France but you did get a two-week vacation, so Toussaint was the greatest thing France had going for it. Mom was taking some time off from work and promised they could watch lots of American movies. Livvie could stay up late and sleep in. She would go down to Cours Mirabeau as much as possible to see what the mime was up to. And best of all, she wouldn't have to deal with school.

Sheila McGrory-Klyza

Chapter 8

"Rise and shine, sleepyhead," Mom said as she pushed open the curtains in Livvie's room. "It's a beautiful day out there. I thought we could go over to le marché and put together a picnic."

One thing Livvie liked about Aix was the market, so this idea roused her from her sleep. Three times a week, practically the entire older part of town was taken over by vendors selling everything from fruits and vegetables to cheese to Italian shoes to skimpy lingerie. Livvie didn't usually get to go because it took place while she was at school. But on a rare free day, she loved wandering through the outdoor stalls, sampling olives or bits of calissons, a soft, almond candy.

They skipped breakfast and decided to pick up a croissant at their favorite boulangerie. Livvie could smell the buttery pastries even before they turned onto the street.

"Why don't you try to order for us," Mom said. "It'll be good practice."

"No way."

"You're never going to learn French if you don't even try to speak it. Monsieur Simon says your written work is coming along well, but you never open your mouth in class."

"There's hardly any chance. He's always the one up there talking."

"Well, here's an opportunity to try. C'mon, just say, 'Bonjour, Madame. Deux croissants, s'il vous plaît,'" Mom whispered, then turned to gaze at the quiches in the glass case as if they were the most interesting thing in the world.

It was their turn to order and the woman at the counter looked at Livvie impatiently.

"Mademoiselle?" the woman said, glaring.

Livvie blurted out as quickly as she could, "Bonjour, Madame. Deux croissants, s'il vous plaît."

"Deux croissants?"

"Oui."

The woman slipped the crescent rolls into a bag, while Mom stepped back over and gave her the money. Livvie was relieved she didn't have to deal with that part too. The large, colorful Euro bills still looked like play money to her. And coins being worth dollars was way too confusing. The woman handed her the bag and said, "Merci, Mademoiselle."

Livvie repeated it back to her, but Mom quickly jumped in and said, "Merci, Madame. Excusez-nous. Au revoir."

"See, I told you I'd mess it up," Livvie said when they were back outside.

"You did great. I love it when people call me Mademoiselle. But she's obviously over fifty so she's a madame. At least you tried. The more you try, the easier it'll become. Of course you'll make mistakes. I still do and I studied French for years. The other day I asked Monsieur Cantini if he knows who steals bikes in town."

"Mom!"

"It wasn't a big deal. He knew I meant sells. The words are similar in French and I'd just gotten them mixed up. I think he thought I was a little nutty but we both laughed about it." Suddenly Mom stopped and pointed. "Look at these gorgeous grapes."

By then they were at Place des Prêcheurs, the square with the big, official-looking buildings. On a market day it became a sea of tables piled high with all kinds of food— fruits and vegetables in every color, mounds of earthy mushrooms, juicy roasted chickens and fresh eggs, baskets of herbs and spices. The blind man who sold his own olive oil was in his usual spot by the fountain calling out to shoppers to come taste his oil. There were red-cheeked farmers selling handmade goat cheese and bakers with stacks of bread in all shapes and sizes.

Mom bought the grapes and then stopped to pick up a baguette. In all the confusion of Livvie's ordering, they had forgotten to get one earlier at the bakery. They sampled some salty tapenade, and chose a garlicky green one made from local olives. Into their basket they piled a few ripe, smelly cheeses, the smellier the better as far as Mom was concerned. And some nougat for dessert.

"Let's stop by that soap vendor," Mom said. "I need a few bars."

The table was covered with a rainbow of soaps, each color bearing a different scent. Livvie picked up a pale purple one and brought it to her nose.

"Which ones should we get? Do you like this one?" Mom sniffed a pink one.

Livvie held hers out to Mom. She inhaled and smiled. "Ah, lavender. Heavenly. We'll take two of those," she said to the man in French.

He was an older man and wore a wool cap with a feather in it. He put three soaps in a bag, said something, and smiled. After Mom paid him, Livvie asked, "Why did he give us three? What did he say?"

"He said he put in an extra one for the jolie fille, or pretty girl. Wasn't that sweet?"

Livvie had to admit it was sweet. And it wasn't the first time someone had given them a little gift at the market. Mom was always coming home with herbs she had never tried before that a vendor had tucked in her bag. Or a perfectly ripe pear needing to be eaten that very day. Livvie doubted this would ever happen at a typical American grocery store, and probably not even at many American farmers markets either.

Their picnic basket was full so they made their way over to the park. It was about a fifteen-minute walk away, on the other side of town. Back in Vermont they would have driven, but in France they didn't have a car. So they wound their way leisurely through the market, the produce stalls gradually merging with a carnival of clothing and jewelry vendors. Tablecloths in sunny, floral prints fluttered in the breeze, and piles of musty, old books beckoned collectors. Every so often there was a vendor selling skimpy underwear, which somehow didn't seem as out of place as Livvie would have thought.

Mom stopped at a table and picked up a lacy, red bra.

"What do you think, Liv? Is it me?" She held it up.

Before Livvie could answer, Mom put it down and said, "Maybe your dad would have stayed if I'd worn something like that every day."

It was the first Mom had mentioned Dad in a while. And the first time she had said anything specific about why they had split up. The only reason she ever gave was "we had grown apart," whatever that meant. Livvie knew Mom talked to him on the phone at night sometimes after she thought Livvie was asleep. She could tell it was him because Mom's voice always sounded tense and she mentioned the house and the bank account. Livvie talked to him every other week, and they emailed almost every day. They wrote about day-to-day stuff, like a baseball game he had gone to or something silly Clover did, or Livvie would tell him about some embarrassing thing that had happened at school. He never said anything about why he and Mom had split up either.

"Isn't this a lovely day?" Mom's question brought Livvie back from her thoughts. "I love how warm it is here, even in late October. Still being able to eat outside is such a treat, isn't it?"

The soft light and silky, warm breeze did feel nice on Livvie's skin. Back in Vermont, the days would have been getting much chillier by now and most of the leaves would have fallen. Here, the trees were still full and the leaves were just showing the slightest hint of changing. She missed the foliage, though, especially the sugar maples with their brilliant reds and oranges. Annabel had sent Livvie a few leaves that she had taped up to her bedroom window.

"Yeah, it's okay," Livvie finally said.

When they got to Cours Mirabeau, Livvie looked around for the mime. She didn't see him today, and the spot under the tree where his box usually stood was empty. People stepped around it though, as if he was there.

A few days before, he had been there. Livvie had sat on the front steps of Monoprix and watched him while Mom ran errands. He had done some goofy poses for a group of young children, making them squeal with laughter. Livvie had kept hoping Malika would appear, standing quietly behind the children. Livvie had pictured herself getting up and walking over and standing beside Malika. Maybe even trying to talk to her.

"Let's cross here," Mom said, taking Livvie's arm.

They waited for a break in the traffic and stepped into the street, walking past Livvie's favorite fountain right in the center of Cours Mirabeau. It was called "Old Mossy" because the entire fountain was covered with lush, green moss. Its water came from a warm spring, and on cool mornings steam rose in a cloud around it. Whenever Livvie passed the fountain, she dipped her hand in the warm water. It reminded her of hiking in the Green Mountains back home.

When they got to the park, they chose a spot near where some old men were playing boules and spread out their blanket. The shiny, metal balls softly clacked against each other as the men tossed them into the dusty court. They cheered and patted each other on the back when someone made a good throw.

Since it was school vacation, the park was pretty crowded, mostly with mothers and children. They streamed by as Livvie and Mom ate their lunch, the children's voices calling out in their lilting, singsong French. A woman walked by holding a little boy's hand. She was dressed in a dark skirt and long-sleeved blouse, and her hair was covered by a draping headscarf. Similar to the kind Malika's mother wore. Livvie nibbled on some grapes, waiting until she had passed, and asked, "Why do Muslim women wear those headscarves?"

"It's part of their religion. So a lot of them wear it because of their religious beliefs. Some other women I think choose to wear it because of their political beliefs. To show their support of Islam. And for some, it's probably a part of their identity. There was a big debate in France several years ago about whether to allow girls to wear them to public school and it was decided they can't."

"Why?" Livvie watched the woman help the boy up onto a swing.

"The French government believes there should be a separation between church and state. It's similar to the US, but a little stricter. They call it laïcité. The idea is that religion should be kept out of public institutions, like schools. It came about when the French monarchy ended, to get away from the power the Catholic Church used to have when France had a king."

"Then why are there saints and crosses all over the place, like even on top of Sainte Victoire?"

"They've been there for a long time. They're just part of the country's cultural history. The law that was passed saying religious symbols aren't allowed in public schools was mainly aimed at the girls wearing headscarves." Mom held out a piece of bread for Livvie.

"That doesn't seem right." Livvie shook her head at the bread and thought about Malika. "How old are the girls when they start to wear them?"

"I don't know, maybe around thirteen or fourteen. So it wouldn't be a concern in your school. Besides, there aren't many Muslims at your school. They mostly live in poor areas and there aren't many poor neighborhoods in Aix. I think it's more of an issue in bigger cities, like Paris and Marseille where there are lots of immigrants from North Africa, especially Algeria."

"Why are there lots of immigrants from there?"

"It used to be a French colony. Then there was a war between France and Algeria in the '50s and '60s and Algeria won its independence."

"Is there a lot of prejudice against Muslims?" Livvie watched the little boy laugh and kick his legs as the woman pushed him on the swing.

"Yeah, I think so. Discrimination is against the law but unfortunately, because of prejudice, Muslims aren't always treated equally. A lot of people associate them with terrorism. Even though it's only a small group of Muslims who are terrorists."

"It must be hard to be a Muslim."

"Yeah, most of them are probably good people who want to live their lives in peace like anybody else."

Like Malika and her mother, Livvie thought. Maybe that was why she didn't have any friends at school. She wasn't new this year, Livvie was certain. She had probably been at the school for a while, but she was as much of an outsider as Livvie was. Livvie wondered if she was as lonely too.

Livvie hadn't been raised in any particular religion, although if someone asked her she would probably say she was a Christian. Her family celebrated Christmas and Easter, and they usually went to church on those holidays. But not regularly on Sundays. Mom and Dad had both been raised as Catholics, but they said they didn't want to force anything on her like it was forced on them. So Livvie didn't feel strongly one way or another about religion.

She didn't understand how some people could be so passionate about it. Her cousins Tyler and Graham in Missouri were that way. Their whole family was really involved in their church. Her Uncle Rob and Aunt Ginny led Sunday school, and both her cousins sang in the choir. It wasn't a Catholic church though. It was some kind of Protestant church. When Livvie's family visited them, their whole weekend revolved around what was going on at their church.

Once, Tyler had asked her why she didn't go to church on Sundays. Livvie didn't know what to say, but he had looked at her as if there was something wrong with her. And another time at Thanksgiving, they were all sitting around her cousins' big dining room table when Dad and Uncle Rob had gotten into an argument about saying grace. Uncle Rob said something about how it was his house and they would say grace the way he wanted to. Dad had stayed quiet for about a half an hour afterwards, which was unusual for him. Livvie couldn't figure out what he was so upset about, but it felt like a gray cloud hung over the rest of the meal. Even during dessert. All over a stupid, little disagreement.

Chapter 9

The vacation flew by. Mom kept her promise and they watched a bunch of American movies. They took a train to Arles and explored the Roman ruins there, wandering through the dusty, crumbling structures, marveling about how they were two thousand years old. They spent a day in Marseille also, a big city on the Mediterranean about a half hour away from Aix. Even though it was nearby, it was totally different from Aix. Walking down la Canebière, one of the main boulevards, they were surrounded by masses of people from around the world. Livvie had gotten so used to hearing French all the time that the other languages jumped out at her, languages she had never heard before. The faces and clothing were all so diverse too. Men in colorful tunics, lots of women wearing headscarves, and teenagers wearing barely anything at all.

As they wandered around the city's old port, they gazed past the ancient forts guarding the entrance and out to the sparkling, turquoise sea.

"Where are all these ships from?" Livvie asked.

"All over the world. Marseille has one of the biggest ports on the Mediterranean. It's a city of immigrants, like New York." Mom pointed out to the sea. "North Africa is right across the water."

Livvie couldn't believe Africa was that close. Back in Vermont, Africa had seemed as far away as Mars.

"I'd like to go to Africa sometime," Livvie said to Mom as they ate bouillabaisse, a spicy fish stew, at one of the portside cafés.

"I would too. There are lots of places I'd like to explore with you."

At that moment, sitting with Mom in a café in Marseille, living in France wasn't too bad. Livvie felt like an adventurer, an explorer, discovering new worlds. At least worlds that were new to her. But before she knew it, it was early November and the vacation was coming to an end.

As she climbed into bed Sunday night, the old familiar pit grew in her stomach. Would school ever get easier? Would she ever be comfortable there? Back home, everybody in her grade knew her. She had lots of friends. Here, she was like the mime down on Cours Mirabeau. School was going on around her but she was completely separate from it.

Livvie wondered if Malika felt the same way, sitting there on the bench at school isolated from all the other girls. Even though she spoke French. Did Malika look for the mime too, every time she went down to the Cours? Maybe she had even talked to him, or knew something about him. Livvie had started carrying a little change in her pocket, so if he was there in front of the café she could drop it in his bowl. She hadn't done it yet, but was ready for the next time she saw him.

The following morning before she left for school, Livvie did something that would change everything. She grabbed one of her favorite novels from her bookshelf and stuffed it in her backpack. This in itself wasn't unusual, but she had a plan: the book would be there if she wanted to bring it out with her for recess. If she decided to go sit down on the bench with Malika.

Livvie debated about it in her head all morning and finally figured, what did she have to lose? When she stepped out into the courtyard after lunch, she was ready. The bench was empty and Malika was nowhere around, but that was okay. Livvie could relax and read on her own. Maybe Malika would come out and join her. She sat down to one side of the bench, leaving some room. Then she opened up her book and settled into the first chapter, familiar as some comfy slippers. Why hadn't she done this before?

The voices of the CM2s faded away as she lost herself in the English words. But she wasn't even at the bottom of the first page when some feet walked up, crunching the gravel in front of the bench. Livvie recognized the feet in their plain brown shoes. They paused, turned, and approached the other end of the bench. The owner of the feet, Malika, sat down. When Livvie looked up and glanced over, Malika gave her a slight smile. Then she opened up her own book. They read quietly to themselves like that for the whole hour.

Livvie brought the book back every day for the next few weeks and joined Malika on the bench at recess. Neither one ever spoke. They just smiled to acknowledge each other and began to read. Sometimes one of them would clear her throat or yawn, but mostly they were quiet. At first it felt awkward to Livvie, sitting there reading quietly to themselves. But before long it became comfortable and the hour passed quickly.

As the days went by, even though they had started out sitting at opposite ends of the bench, they both gradually moved closer to the middle. So after a few weeks, they were sitting side by side. Maybe it was because it had gotten chillier and they were trying to keep themselves warm. But Livvie didn't think so. Sometimes their elbows brushed against each other as they each turned a page. They read at about the same pace, so Livvie tried to synchronize it. Tried to make their elbows touch. She thought Malika tried to also.

Chapter 10

Mom's birthday was coming up soon. She had turned forty last year and it was a big deal for her. She said turning forty was a milestone, kind of like turning thirteen and becoming a teenager, but not as exciting. When Livvie asked her what milestone it marked, she said, "Middle age, the last hurrah."

Livvie wasn't sure what that meant exactly, but she had caught Mom plucking out her gray hairs in the bathroom with the tweezers. There were also all these new bottles of face cream on the table by the sink. And a few pieces of fancy lingerie had been hanging on the drying rack lately. Some tiny underwear and lacy black bras.

Just the other afternoon, Mom had come home with darker hair. Her hair was usually plain brown. Not dark brown or light brown, plain brown. The same color as her eyes. It was straight like Livvie's and, for as long as Livvie could remember, she had worn it to her shoulders. Mostly back in a ponytail or barrette. When Mom stepped in the door with her new hair, Livvie hardly recognized her. It was shorter, much shorter in the back but longer toward her chin, and dark brown. The color of dark chocolate.

"Mom!" Livvie said, "What did you do to your hair?"

"Don't you love it? I dyed it. And isn't this a great cut? Pascal says it's très chic."

"Who's Pascal?"

"The guy who cut it. I can take you for a new 'do if you want. He's really funny and speaks a little English."

Livvie had to admit her hair did look good. It made her look like she was dressed up, even if she was wearing jeans. But Livvie liked her own hair the way it was. For the past few years she had worn it a little past her shoulders, and she would never dye it. It was light brown or dark blond, depending on how you looked at it. Mom called it honey brown. Dad's hair was the same color. He had green eyes, though, not blue. "Eyes like blue sea glass" was how Dad described hers. When she was little at the beach, he would help her try to find pieces of sea glass that matched all of their eyes. Livvie used to think it was cool how the three of them had completely different colored eyes, but not anymore.

"No thanks, Mom. But your hair looks good. It makes you look French," Livvie said.

"Thanks, ma chèrie."

Mom did look French. She was small-boned and slender, like most French women. When Livvie was little, she used to think Mom was the most beautiful woman in the world. But at some point she had begun to see her differently. That her skin was sort of blotchy and she had a lot of wrinkles around her eyes, especially when she was tired. It was around the same time Livvie realized Mom could be wrong about things. Important things. And sometimes she made big mistakes.

Mom was pretty though. She had a narrow, oval face and small features. Livvie's face was wider, like Dad's. Mom said she could tell Livvie was going to be bigger than she was, and already Livvie could wear some of her sweaters if she cuffed up the sleeves. It wouldn't be long before she could wear her pants. Back home, Livvie was about average height for her class, but in France she was one of the tallest. She towered over these petite French girls, and even some of the boys. It didn't help that she was a year older than all of them. They probably thought she had been held back in the US and was just a big, dumb American.

Another thing was different about Mom—she was smoking again. She used to smoke before Livvie was born, but gave it up when she got pregnant. But lately, after Livvie went to bed, Mom would go sit on the balcony and smoke. Outside Livvie's window, the tip of Mom's cigarette glowed red in the dark like an angry firefly.

Livvie hated smoking. She felt like screaming at Mom through the window, "Don't you know how bad that is for you? Who's the grownup here?" But instead she stared at the burning firefly trapped in its arcing pattern until it faded and burned out.

On Mom's birthday, Livvie decided to shop for something after school. For the past month she had been walking home by herself and was on her own until Mom got back from work, so she had a little time. She had a key to the apartment and would have a snack and do her homework until Mom came home around 5:30. Her office was only a ten-minute walk away, and the Durands were usually in their apartment if Livvie ever needed anything. Not that she wanted to hang out with the Durands. When Mom had finally dragged her down to their apartment so they could introduce themselves, Madame Durand had looked Livvie up and down as if she was evaluating her cleanliness and her husband had cowered behind her like she was some kind of commander.

To shop for Mom's present, Livvie headed toward Place des Prêcheurs, looking in the store windows along the way. Everything was a lot more than she could afford. Usually she and Dad would pick something out for Mom together. Like a birdhouse, or a pair of earrings. But Livvie didn't have enough money for something like that with her small allowance. She passed the flower shop with its buckets of cheerful blossoms out in front. Flowers! Mom loved flowers. She said gardening was one of the few things she missed from home. And they couldn't be too expensive.

Livvie examined the choices in the buckets. There were lots of different colors and shapes, but she remembered Mom liked roses. She had several bushes back home. And Dad used to get them for her on special occasions. Livvie picked out a small bouquet of pink rosebuds, barely opened, and a card with balloons on the front.

At the counter, she handed the saleswoman ten Euro and got a few coins back as change. Livvie glanced at them to make sure the change was correct before putting it away.

When she got home, she put the roses into a vase on the table and sat down with the card. She started to write "Happy birthday, Mom!" but crossed it out and put "Bon Anniversaire, Maman!" instead. Livvie knew this would make her happy. She had just finished writing "Je t'aime" and signing her name when the key turned in the door.

"Hi, Liv," Mom called out, like usual.

"Hi, I'm in here."

When Mom came in the doorway, she stopped and gasped. "Sweetie, they're beautiful."

"Happy Birthday, Mom. There's a card too."

Mom slid the card from its envelope and read it. When she looked up, her eyes were all watery. Livvie couldn't tell if she was happy or sad. Then she leaned down to kiss Livvie on both cheeks, giving her the French bises. Lately she had been doing this before Livvie went to bed, instead of her usual hug and kiss goodnight. But this time Mom stopped after one kiss, threw her arms around Livvie, and hugged her tightly.

"Thank you, Livvie. Je t'aime aussi."

Chapter 11

One day in late November, after a few weeks of reading on the bench together, Malika was absent. Livvie sat down on the cold bench anyway and opened up her book. The strong mistral winds whipped around her and she shivered. The gusts picked up particles of sand that stung her cheeks and worked their way into her jacket. She glanced at her watch. Fifty-two more minutes. She wished Malika was there. It was much more comfortable when she was sitting there too. Even if they didn't talk.

They had begun sitting together at lunch also. Even though they never spoke, it wasn't as weird as Livvie thought it would be. It was like she was sitting with a friend. Livvie would sometimes pass Malika the serving spoon or Malika would fill up Livvie's glass of water. They didn't interact much in the classroom, but for some reason Livvie didn't feel so alone there either. Malika sat on the other side of the room and was usually absorbed in her schoolwork, but Livvie liked seeing her over there.

Malika was absent for several days, and when she came back she had a cough. She bundled up at recess, though, and joined Livvie on the bench. Livvie gave her a bigger smile than usual and pulled her coat up close to her neck, saying "Brrrrrrr." Malika smiled and nodded, pointed to her throat, and coughed a little. Livvie tried to make a sympathetic face, turning the corners of her mouth down like a clown. Malika laughed and said something Livvie didn't understand. But she recognized a word that sounded like meem. Meem … that must be how mime was pronounced in French because their long i sounded like the English long e.

"Mime! … Cours Mirabeau … Mime!" Livvie put her elbow on her knee and her chin on her hand, imitating the mime's Thinker pose.

"Oui!" Malika said, nodding and smiling. Then she did The Thinker pose too.

They both burst out laughing. Next, Livvie pointed to Malika's book and, using facial expressions, asked her if it was happy or sad. Malika made her eyes droop and her lips quiver, but she hugged the book to her heart. Pointing to Livvie's book, she asked her the same thing. Livvie imitated Malika's sad face, followed by a big, cheesy smile, and finally she brought the book to her lips and kissed it. They both laughed again and kept on going, acting out what they were trying to say. Miming. It was easy. Kind of like playing charades. A few times they got so puzzled by what the other one was trying to say that they both burst out in uncontrollable giggles.

The bell suddenly rang and Livvie wished it hadn't. She wished recess would last longer so she and Malika could continue to mime with each other. They didn't need words to be able to communicate, at least about general things. Words would have helped with specifics, but maybe they would have also made it more complicated.

Over the next several days, Livvie learned Malika's favorite animal was a cat too. And that she loved ice cream and swimming. And reading, but Livvie knew that already. She learned the woman Livvie had seen meeting Malika after school was her mom as Livvie had guessed. And that Malika was an only child too. Livvie learned so much about her and they hadn't ever even had a real conversation.

After this, as hard as it was for Livvie to believe, she no longer dreaded going to school. The stomachaches at night weren't as bad, and lunch and recess became her favorite part of the day. In class in the mornings, she caught herself glancing at the clock to see how much longer she had to wait until lunch. How much longer until she could mime with Malika.

It was around this time also that Monsieur began teaching English lessons to the class. Livvie and Peahead were his assistants. Mostly they repeated what he said, silly sentences such as, "I like to sing. I don't like to go skiing." Since she and Peahead had different accents, Monsieur wanted the class to hear both the British and the American way of speaking. At first Livvie thought it would be embarrassing, but it wasn't. It was actually fun to correct the class's pronunciation after months of being so nervous about speaking at school.

Maybe it was because of the English lessons, but some of the students were paying a little more attention to Livvie. She almost choked on her beef stew when the Chipies all sat down near her at lunch. Nicole fluffed out her long, auburn hair and said, "Salut, Olivia." Malika was sitting across from Livvie, but Nicole didn't say anything to her.

When Livvie said "Salut" back to Nicole, she smiled, although her eyes didn't. She turned to Sylvie and Pilar and they chatted among themselves, sometimes glancing Livvie's way and saying "Oui?"

Livvie smiled back and nodded since she couldn't follow the conversation. Malika sat across from her, not saying anything. Why was that? Had something happened between her and these girls? Livvie wished she could ask her.

If only she could speak their language. She was beginning to understand a few words here and there. Certain words would stand out and she would recognize them clearly. But there were still a lot of words that just blended together in one long jabber of nonsense-sounding syllables. Reading was better. Mom had helped her translate the reading assignments at first, but recently Livvie had been doing it on her own. She kept the dictionary right beside her and had to look up a lot of words, but little by little it was getting easier. She hoped this meant that soon she would be able to read in French. And understand what people were saying. And actually speak it herself. Then she could really talk with Malika. She could find out why she was so quiet.

Chapter 12

"What do you want to do to celebrate Thanksgiving?" Mom asked Livvie over dinner. "It's this Thursday."

What Livvie wanted to do was fly to her cousins in Missouri like they did every year. They would all play touch football out on their lawn and stuff themselves silly on a huge meal. But she said instead, "I don't know. I have school like any other day."

"The two of us could still have a nice dinner. We could go out to a restaurant if you'd like."

"No, that would make it seem even less like Thanksgiving. I'd rather eat at home."

"Thanksgiving is a hard one here because it's such an American holiday. Nobody else celebrates it. I don't think we could even find a turkey to roast. Some Americans from the office are getting together at La Rotonde though. We could join them if you want. They're ex-pats like us."

Ex-pat? Was that what she was? Whatever that meant. "Would I be the only kid?"

"Probably. Nobody else in the group has kids, at least around your age. They're either all grown up or still babies."

The thought of hanging out with Mom's friends at some fancy restaurant didn't sound like much fun. They were all nice, but Livvie had gone out with them once before and they had gotten some wine and laughed like lunatics while Livvie sat there bored with her Shirley Temple.

"I think I'd rather stay home. I have a history test the next day anyway."

"That's fine. We don't have to go. I'll pick you up from school tomorrow and we can go shopping together for the meal."

The next day, Mom met her at the gate at 4:30 and they headed over to Monoprix. As they were turning onto Cours Mirabeau, Livvie spied the mime's box in its usual place, but it was empty. She wondered where he could be, where he went when he took his little breaks. Then, as they got closer and were passing the café near his spot, Livvie saw him. He was sitting at one of the tables with a coffee cup in front of him. He had on his silver paint and white costume, but he looked completely different. His face was relaxed and he was gazing out at the stream of people going by just like anybody else. Livvie realized she was staring at him, because his eyes met hers. He gave her a little smile and nod, like he recognized her. She smiled and nodded back.

"He was sitting at a café today," Livvie said to Mom as they went through Monoprix's front doors.

"Who was?" Mom slipped her phone back in her purse.

"The mime."

"Oh. Maybe since there are fewer tourists around now he's able to take more breaks. He probably gets pretty chilly being out on the sidewalk all day. So what do you want to have for our big feast?"

"I wonder what color his skin is under the silver paint."

"Hmm. What do you think of mashed potatoes and green beans with roasted chicken? I can pick up a chicken on Thursday afternoon. I don't think we'll be able to find cranberries, but I could make a dried cherry chutney. How does that sound?"

"Fine," Livvie sighed. She wished she could talk with the mime. She wondered if he was French. Or maybe he was from another country and didn't speak the language either. Maybe he even spoke English. What would she ask him? Did he like being a mime? How did he learn it? Why did he paint his skin silver and not some other color?

"And for dessert, how about apple tart from our bakery? It's even better than apple pie. What do you think?"

"Sounds great, Mom."

As they left Monoprix, the mime was back on the sidewalk. He was standing in front of his box and had one of his white arms curved as if he was holding something. The other silver hand gently petted the air. It looked like he was holding an animal. A cat? A dog? Suddenly he jumped as if he had been bitten. The small audience broke into laughter and one of them snapped a photo. Livvie fell a few steps behind Mom so she didn't notice Livvie had stopped. She reached in her pocket and dropped a few coins in his bowl. He gave her another nod and she looked him straight in the eyes. He looked straight back. His eyes were medium brown, and looked warm and alive among all that silver and white.

Thanksgiving ended up being disappointing like Livvie expected. Since they usually had roast chicken once a week, it was nothing special. Mom tried to make it fancier with candles and linen napkins, but it didn't feel at all like a holiday. Midway through the meal, she got up and put on some music. She said it was to add to the fancy atmosphere, but Livvie knew she put it on so it wouldn't be so quiet. Even the apple tart, which was usually one of Livvie's favorite desserts, didn't help.

After dinner she called Dad who was at Uncle Rob and Aunt Ginny's. Aunt Ginny answered the phone and Livvie could tell she was trying hard to sound cheery. But her usually honeyed, southern accent sounded stiff and fake. When Livvie was talking to Dad, she could hear a football game on in the background and the cheers of her cousins and uncle. She could picture all of them in their big, vaulted family room with a warm fire in the fireplace. Because of the six hour time difference, their turkey would still be in the oven, filling the whole house with its cozy holiday aroma. Someone in the background let out an excited whoop. Even though Livvie usually had no interest in watching football, her heart ached. She missed her family, she missed their traditions, she missed her country. When she handed the phone to Mom for her quick hello, Livvie was fighting back tears.

She went into her room and walked over to the window. The sun was setting and the jagged outline of Sainte Victoire was black and ominous against the gray sky.

Livvie closed the curtains and sat down on her bed. It was chilly in her room and she shivered, wishing Clover was lying beside her purring. Across the room on her dresser, he was curled up on her old bed. In a cold photo. Next to another cold photo of Dad on their front porch. And another of Annabel, Sarah, and Kendall at the lake.

Livvie tried to distract herself by pulling out her history notebook. The test was on the history of Aix, and she was supposed to learn a long list of different cultures that had lived in the region. At least Monsieur Simon said she could use her dictionary and have some extra time if she needed it. She stared at the page. The words and dates swam. What did she care about the Celtic-Ligurians, the Romans, the Teutons, the Ambrons, the Christians, the Visigoths, the Lombards, the Maures, the Counts of Barcelona, and the French monarchy? Who were those people and what did any of them have to do with her life? What use would she ever have for knowing about their cultures? Their ruins?

Her eyes stung. Footsteps clicked in the tiled foyer and she wished she had closed her door. Mom came into the room, but Livvie kept staring at her notebook.

"I know it's hard, Liv," Mom said. "I'm sorry Thanksgiving wasn't more special."

"Yeah." Livvie kept her head down.

Mom sat on the bed beside her and put her arm around Livvie's shoulders. "Christmas will be better, I promise. They really do it up here, with lights, and carolers, and a huge Christmas market. And I haven't told you this yet because I wanted it to be a surprise, but Grandma is planning to come visit us."

At this news, Livvie looked up. The idea of seeing a familiar face from back home warmed her all over. "She is?"

"That's the plan. She's coming a couple days before Christmas and is staying for a whole week."

Livvie reached over and hugged Mom back. "I'm so glad."

"Me too," Mom said, her voice cracking. "Sometimes even moms need their moms."

Chapter 13

Mom was right about something for once. In Aix they really did celebrate Christmas in a big way. Before November was over, crews were out hanging decorations all over town. Colorful lights twinkled in the trees, garlands draped across the narrow streets, a giant French flag made out of blue, white, and red lights festooned the front of city hall, and a huge canopy of white lights covered the length of Cours Mirabeau.

A Christmas market was set up along the Cours also, with little wooden chalets lining the street. The vendors sold handmade jewelry, wooden toys, pottery, and santons—clay figurines in traditional Provençal costumes used to create elaborate crèches. And at the far end of the Cours, near the giant fountain, there was an actual carnival, with rides and games. And even cotton candy, which they called barbe à Papa. Back in Vermont Livvie had only been to carnivals in the summertime, but in Aix it was mild enough to have one in December.

At school, a Christmas tree appeared in the hallway outside Livvie's classroom. It was decorated with red and green balls and had a silver star on top. Livvie didn't remember ever having a tree at school back home. And she was surprised to see one in France because she didn't think there were supposed to be any religious symbols in French public schools. Especially given that big debate Mom had mentioned about Muslim girls wearing headscarves to school. When Livvie asked Mom about the tree, she said the French probably considered the decorations to be a secular holiday tradition, not religious. And not necessarily Christian. But that didn't make sense to Livvie. And how must it have made Malika feel?

Livvie decided to do some research on Muslim holidays on the Internet. She learned about Eid-ul-Fitr, which had taken place a few weeks before and was one of their biggest religious celebrations. It followed the month of Ramadan, a time of fasting when Muslims prayed about their holy book, the Koran, being revealed to their Prophet Mohammed. Livvie learned that fasting was when Muslims didn't eat from sunrise to sunset, although kids didn't usually have to. At the end of Ramadan, they celebrated Eid by giving gifts and sharing a big meal with family and friends.

It sounded a lot like Christmas, except for the fasting part. Livvie wondered how Malika felt celebrating her big holiday without anyone in the school acknowledging it. And now she was surrounded by Christmas trees and Santas and manger scenes all over town. Did that make her sad or mad or just plain lost?

Even though Ramadan and Eid were over, she decided to make Malika a card. She copied the image of the star and crescent from the website on the front of the card and drew some presents around it. Unsure of what to put inside, she kept it simple and wrote "Bon Ramadan" and signed her name. The next day she brought the card to school and at lunch handed it across the table to Malika. She opened it with a puzzled expression, and then a big smile spread across her face.

When Malika looked up, she said "merci" and something in a language Livvie didn't recognize. It sounded like "shukran." And then "thank you" in English. She stood the card up on the table between them and during the whole meal kept glancing down at it, her smile lighting her eyes.

The weeks leading up to Christmas became a blur of studying for tests, decorating for the holidays, and getting ready for Grandma's visit. In her quest to make the apartment festive, Mom came home all excited one day to have found real mistletoe at the market. She hung a wreath on the door and their stockings by the fireplace. The two stockings looked lonely hanging there by themselves though. Mom must have thought so too, because the next day she came home with another one to put up for Grandma.

One Sunday afternoon, Livvie and Mom walked across town to the tree market to pick out a tree. They were all much smaller than Christmas trees back home, and Mom said they cost a fortune. But a small one was all they had room for in their apartment anyway. They picked out a cute one and carried it back through town, the December sun still warm on Livvie's face. It would be frigid back home at this time and there was probably snow on the ground. There always was when they went to cut down their tree at the McKinleys' tree farm down the road. When Livvie was little, Dad would pull her around on her bright red sled while they all searched for the perfect tree. Afterwards, they would go home and have hot chocolate before putting it up and decorating it.

Shrieks from children on the mini roller coaster at the carnival brought Livvie back to the bustling street scene. They wound through the crowds waiting in line for the giant slide and the bumper cars and started to make their way up Cours Mirabeau.

"Let's go up on the left side," Livvie said to Mom, squinting toward the mime's usual spot.

"It's too crowded. Let's stay to the right."

It definitely was crowded along the left side. Especially in front of the small stage set up toward the other end of the Cours where some carolers were singing. As they got closer, Livvie recognized the music from "Hark the Herald Angels Sing," but the words were in French. She saw the mime too, his box not far from the stage. He must have moved it to be closer to the crowd. He was up on top of the box, pretending to conduct the carolers. His silver hands waved back and forth, holding an imaginary baton. Most of the crowd was focused on the carolers, but a few were more interested in watching him. He hammed it up, as if he was conducting a giant orchestra.

Livvie wondered if he celebrated Christmas. Or Eid, or Chanukah, or some other holiday. Or maybe nothing. She wondered if he felt strongly about his religion, or if he was like her. Possibly, though, she would feel strongly about being a Christian and celebrating her holidays if she lived in a place that didn't celebrate them at all.

She had a few coins in her pocket and wished she could put some in his bowl. But both her hands were gripping the trunk of their tree, and Mom was marching forward without any intention of stopping. Livvie tried to catch the mime's eye from across the street. He was facing her, waving his baton and nodding in time to the music. Their eyes met and he winked. Not a slight wink from a bit of dust in his eye, but a full-fledged wink. Livvie was sure of it.

When she and Mom got to their door, Livvie could finally put the tree down for a rest. Mom searched around for her key while Livvie studied the smiley face. It was winking too. Or maybe the artist had been in a hurry and drew a line for one of the eyes. Either way, Livvie had never noticed that before.

They lugged the tree up the stairs and stood it in the living room. Mom made hot chocolate and put on some Christmas music. She sang along to "Jingle Bells" as she unwrapped the ornaments. They were only able to pack a few favorites to bring along to France, so the tree still looked bare after they hung them on.

"Don't worry, we can pick up some more ornaments at the Christmas market," Mom said. "How about if we pop popcorn and make old-fashioned garlands?"

"I have homework," Livvie said and headed into her bedroom. It was partially true, because she did have some reading to do. But in reality school had finally eased up after all the recent exams. She guessed Monsieur Simon was now busy working on grades for their report cards. They would get them in a few days, before Christmas vacation.

Livvie had no idea how she would do on her report card. She wasn't too worried about English, of course. Or gym class and art. They were pretty much the same as back home, except for wearing the smock. The same went for math, which had always come easily to her. But in history, literature, and science, with all the reading and writing involved, she had no idea whether she would even pass. She was able to understand more now when reading, but Monsieur still spoke impossibly fast and she wasn't sure how much she comprehended.

Before taking out her homework, Livvie walked over to her window and pushed aside the curtains. The sun was getting low and turning the sky all pink and purple. Ribbons of clouds floated above Sainte Victoire. The mountain itself was purple too. Grayish purple, but more purple than gray. The top didn't look so jagged either. Must have been a trick of light.

Chapter 14

On the last day of school before Christmas break, everyone in Livvie's class was buzzing in that old, familiar pre-holiday spirit. Livvie was excited for the vacation too, but not the way she would have been back home, with all the traditions to look forward to. She and Mom always baked cookies and made a gingerbread house each year and entered it in the town's contest. They had never won, but Livvie loved designing a house and picking out all the candy for it. Their neighbors the Millers always had a bonfire and gave sleigh rides on Christmas Eve. And they always got together with Annabel's family for a big dinner some time during the holidays. She and Annabel would take all month to choose the right gift for each other. This year Livvie had sent her a picture of herself in a frame that had little Eiffel Towers all over it, and a beaded necklace she had found at the market.

Livvie still had a little more shopping to do, but the week before she had gotten a gift for Monsieur. It was up with all the others from the class in a pile on his desk. Livvie had had no idea what to get him, until Mom had suggested maple syrup. They looked for some from Vermont, but the only kind they could find was from Canada. At least it was from the same continent, as Mom had said. Livvie had also made him a card using her best French cursive, trying hard to write in their graceful, looping script.

At lunch, everyone's excitement was simmering. Even the servers smiled and joked as they placed down the steaming platters of food. There was a special dessert of frosted chocolate cake, and when it was time for recess, the class burst out onto the courtyard like it was Christmas morning itself. The boys raced over to the football area, and the Chipies linked arms as they formed their circle, their laughter bouncing off the building's walls like a handful of superballs.

After being jostled through the doors in the crush of other students, Livvie and Malika walked over to the bench together as they had been doing for some time. When they sat down though, instead of opening her book, Malika handed it to Livvie. She took it and looked at Malika, not knowing what she was expected to do.

"It's for you," Malika said in French. "A gift."

Livvie clearly understood what Malika had said, and she didn't know whether she was more surprised that she understood Malika so easily, or because of the gift itself.

"Merci beaucoup," Livvie said. She continued in French, "It's really nice."

Livvie ran her hand over the familiar creased cover and opened it. Malika's name was written on the inside in faded pencil. Malika Nasri. Below her name was her phone number. In darker pencil, more recent. Before she knew what she was doing, Livvie handed Malika her own book. It was one of her old favorites that had gotten worn and bent from its regular travel back and forth to school in her backpack.

"For you," Livvie said, again in French.

Malika took it and smiled, saying, "Merci. Thank you."

And then, maybe because they were sitting there holding books neither one of them could easily read, or maybe because Livvie was ready to try to have a real conversation, in French, they began to talk.

"I'll try to read it over the vacation," Malika said.

"I'll try to read yours too, but my grandma's coming to France for Christmas." Livvie's French faltered but she kept going. "And we'll be doing lots of special things."

"That's nice. Do you miss her?"

"Yes, very much. I miss my whole family. They're all back in the United States."

"I get to see my grandmother a lot. And all my cousins and aunts and uncles. They all live in Marseille so I see them when we go to the mosque."

Malika tucked a strand of hair behind her ear and looked down at the book in her lap.

"You're lucky. What's a mosque?"

"It's where we worship. Like a church. I go every week with my parents."

"My dad lives in the US too. So I don't get to see him either. They're ... divorced." Livvie said the last word quickly. It was the first time she had said it out loud.

"You live here with just your mother?"

"Yeah. She works for a computer company and got a chance to move here. She loves France. So she brought me with her."

"My mom works with computers too. She's an engineer. She's always on her cell phone."

"No way! My mom too!"

They talked like this for the whole recess. Sometimes they had to mime a little when they got stumped, but Livvie was amazed at what she was able to say. Like Mom predicted would happen, something clicked in her brain and words—whole sentences—tumbled out. Livvie could understand most of what Malika said too. When they got confused on a word, they used gestures or other words that meant something similar. And like in a game show, they both got all excited when they figured it out.

When the bell interrupted them, they lingered on the bench a few more moments before picking up their gifts to join the others.

Chapter 15

"Diane, this is charming!" Grandma stepped through the front door, breathless from climbing the stairs. "I wasn't sure about it at first with all that graffiti on the building, but the inside is adorable."

"It's a little small, but we like it, don't we, Liv?" Mom said. "Why don't you show Grandma where your room is since she'll be sleeping in there."

Livvie picked up one of Grandma's bags and carried it into her room. Since she had twin beds, Grandma would be sharing her room.

"Do you feel like lying down before dinner, Mother? You must be tired from the travel," Mom said.

"No, I'm fine. I actually could use a little walk after being on the plane. You know how I hate to sit still for such a long time."

"Livvie, while I get dinner ready, why don't you walk over to the bakery with Grandma. You could pick up a baguette and show her the neighborhood."

"Sure," Livvie said, grabbing her jacket. As she opened up the front door leading to the sidewalk, a motorcycle whizzed by right outside the building.

"My goodness!" Grandma cried. "What is he doing riding on the sidewalk?!"

"Oh, yeah. You need to be careful about the motorcycles here. They don't always stay in the street."

"Careful, indeed. He nearly killed us!"

"You'll get used to it. You can hear them coming from a mile away," Livvie said laughing.

"I would say so." Grandma looked down the sidewalk after the motorcyclist. "Are we going that way too?"

"No, it's this way, around the corner."

As they walked along, Grandma said, "I can see what your mother means—it is a lovely town. The weather reminds me of back home in Phoenix. Beautiful architecture too. It's such a shame about all the ugly graffiti though."

"You know, it's funny, but I don't notice it anymore."

Livvie was surprised to hear herself say it, but it was true. She thought back to her first walk around the town with Mom, and how the motorcycles terrified her, just like Grandma. And the graffiti looked so menacing. But now, it was all part of the scenery of Aix. Livvie even kind of liked some of the graffiti. The colors energized the town. Without the graffiti, the buildings would have looked too bland or formal.

"Watch out for the dog poop!" Livvie yelled, grabbing Grandma's elbow.

"Ugh! Is it always this dirty?"

"Yeah, but like I said, you get used to it."

By this time they were at the bakery and, as they entered, Grandma's face brightened.

"Ohhhhh, this all looks wonderful, Livvie."

"It is wonderful. Mom and I have tried almost everything."

Livvie turned to the woman behind the counter and said, "Bonjour, Madame. Une baguette, s'il vous plaît. Et un pain au chocolat aussi, pour ma grand-mère."

The woman smiled and handed her the bread and chocolate pastry. Livvie counted out the money and gave it to her.

"Merci, Olivia. À bientôt," the woman said.

"Merci, Madame. À bientôt."

Livvie tucked the baguette under her arm and handed the pain au chocolat to Grandma. She stared at Livvie and said, "Olivia, you speak French like a native. You sound more French than your mother!"

"Don't tell her that. She won't be too happy."

"I don't think that's true. She might be a little envious of your accent, especially those beautiful r's, but she's thrilled you're doing so well. You heard her raving about your report card. It's remarkable how well you're doing in school."

"Yeah, I was kind of surprised by my grades."

"You've always been a strong student. But to be able to do well in a foreign country! We're both very proud of you. Your grandpa would be too. He was always much more of a traveler than I am. You are a brave girl, Livvie, you know that?"

Livvie had never thought of herself as brave. But maybe she was. Not in the sense of being a superhero or anything like that. But to be thrown into another culture and have to adapt like she had done did take some courage.

"Yeah, Grandma. I guess I am brave."

"How about if we three gals do a little Christmas shopping this morning?" Mom said the next day as she was pouring tea for Grandma. "We need to celebrate your excellent report card, Livvie. And I got a nice holiday bonus in my paycheck yesterday. Since tomorrow's Christmas Eve, the stores will be too crowded then."

"Sounds good to me," Grandma said. "But I want to have a little time this afternoon to do some baking with Livvie."

"Sure, both sound great," Livvie said. She and Mom had passed by a shop with a big display of Chipie clothes in the window recently. It looked like an expensive store, but Livvie hoped that maybe since it was Christmas Mom would buy a few things for her. "Do you think we could go to that store with the Chipie clothes?"

"I don't see why not, if that's what you'd like. I think we can splurge a bit."

After breakfast, they headed over to the upscale neighborhood where the shop was located. As they pulled open the front door, loud American pop music escaped onto the street. Livvie didn't have anything particular in mind, and began browsing through the tops while Mom and Grandma looked around. The store was crowded with girls and their moms, so Livvie wasn't aware Nicole was there too until a voice behind her said, "Salut, Olivia."

Livvie turned around and saw Nicole standing beside a très chic woman holding a large shopping bag. She had the same auburn hair as Nicole, and the same thick, arching eyebrows.

"So, you're Olivia," the woman said in French. "Nicole has told me so much about you. I'm her mother."

Livvie was stunned by this comment and barely mumbled a reply: "Salut, Nicole. Bonjour, Madame."

"You're American, oui?" Nicole's mother said.

"Oui."

By now Mom and Grandma had come over to join the conversation. "Bonjour, Madame," Mom said, holding out her hand. "I'm Olivia's mother, Diane. And this is Olivia's grandmother, Helen."

"Bonjour, Mesdames. My name is Julie. My daughter talks about Olivia all the time. We must get them together. Perhaps after the holidays?"

"Why, yes, that would be lovely," Mom said in her most precise French. "We'll have the girls arrange something."

As they said their goodbyes, Livvie stood there dumbfounded. She couldn't believe Nicole talked about her at home with her family. She thought Nicole barely noticed her.

"Nicole seems like a nice girl," Mom said after Nicole and her mother had left, another large shopping bag in hand. "Why haven't you ever mentioned her?"

"Because I didn't think she cared one way or another about me. I'm actually pretty shocked she's ever mentioned me to her mother."

"Liv, don't sell yourself short. She obviously wants to be your friend. You should invite her over to the apartment one day after school."

Invite Nicole over to their apartment? That would be too weird. What would they do? What would they talk about? Livvie would much rather invite Malika. She didn't say this to Mom though. In fact she hadn't mentioned anything at all about Malika to Mom yet. Livvie had a feeling Mom wouldn't be so enthusiastic about that friendship.

"I don't know," Livvie said, turning back to the rack of tops and ending the conversation.

Chapter 16

Christmas morning Livvie woke up early like she did every year. It was still dark in the room and she didn't know where she was at first. When she heard Grandma stir in the bed beside her, she remembered and glanced over at the clock. It was 6:30, still too early to wake Mom and Grandma. Since they all had gone to midnight Mass the night before, she had agreed to wait until at least 7:00 to wake them.

Livvie's thoughts drifted back over Christmas Eve. They had gone to a fancy dinner, one with about six different courses. When they left the restaurant, they were completely stuffed, but still had another hour until it was time for Mass. So they decided to go for a walk and began wandering down the Cours. The canopy of lights twinkled above them and some carolers were singing a few blocks away. The crowds that had jammed the street earlier in the day were gone though, probably home with their families.

As they had walked past the spot where the mime usually stood, Livvie had wondered where he was, and if he had a big family to celebrate with. Maybe they were all lingering over the traditional thirteen desserts that Provençal families serve on Christmas Eve. He had been there in the afternoon though. Mom, Grandma, and Livvie had been strolling through the Christmas market one last time when Livvie had spotted him across the street.

"Grandma, come with me for a minute. I want to show you something," Livvie had said.

Mom glanced up from a santons display. "You two go on. I'll be right there."

Livvie led Grandma across the street, saying, "There's this cool mime over here."

"Yes, I saw him the other day with your mother. He was pretending to unwrap some presents. He sure did get the crowd laughing."

They had joined the small audience surrounding the mime and peered past the shoulders of the other onlookers. He was sitting down on his box, rocking an imaginary baby. He held the baby gently to his chest and was gazing down at it lovingly.

"I wonder if he studied with Marcel Marceau. He's a famous French mime, you know. I think he has a mime school in Paris. Wouldn't that be something, going to school to learn how to be a mime?" Grandma had asked.

Livvie had never considered that he may have actually gone to school to learn how to mime. She didn't think of miming as something a person learned, like a language. Anybody could do it. That was one of the things she loved about it. Like when she and Malika had first tried to communicate with each other, and they had mimed because they didn't speak the same language. Miming just came naturally for them. They could understand each other because so much of their body language was shared, because they were both people.

Livvie was lying in bed thinking about all this when she heard Mom's bedroom door open. She glanced at the clock and it was already a little past 7:00. As she climbed out of bed, she said, "Merry Christmas, Grandma! Joyeux Noël!".

"Merry Christmas, Livvie," Grandma said, yawning. "I'm not even going to try it in French at this hour."

"Joyeux Noël, ma chèrie," Mom said from the doorway. "Let's go see what Père Noël brought."

Maybe because the tree was so little, or maybe because Mom was being extra generous this year, the presents looked like they were overflowing. They all took turns unwrapping gifts, but Mom and Grandma insisted that Livvie do two at a time. She got a few books, mostly in English, but some in French. She also got lots of Chipie things, some she had picked out earlier with Mom and some surprises, including one of those sleek schoolbags in navy blue. There was a Chipie pencil case and other Chipie school supplies in her stocking. Grandma gave Livvie a silver charm bracelet, "to fill up with memories," she said. The first charm on it was a tiny heart engraved with "Love from Grandma."

Mom was happy with the perfume Livvie had picked out for her with Grandma. And Grandma loved the silk scarf Livvie had chosen for her with Mom. "Maybe now I can pass for French," Grandma said laughing, draping it elaborately over her nightgown.

Dad's present had arrived a few days earlier, but Livvie had put it under the tree to save for Christmas morning. When she unwrapped it and lifted it out of its box, tears came to her eyes. It was a gray and white stuffed cat that looked like Clover. Livvie hugged it and blinked hard, remembering when they had first gotten Clover. Livvie was six, and one day he showed up in the field beside their house. He was jumping around in the tall grass, batting at a red clover blossom. Livvie begged to keep him. Dad was easy to convince, but they both had to work on Mom for a few days.

"Dad's going to call this afternoon," Mom said. "He has a surprise for you."

Mom wouldn't tell Livvie what it was, so she tried not to get her hopes up too much. If he and Mom were getting back together, surely Mom would have told her. But maybe he was surprising Mom too.

Livvie opened Annabel's present next. It had come a few days earlier also, but Livvie had forced herself to wait until Christmas like they always did back home. It was a DVD and, as soon as Livvie opened it, she ran over to the TV to put it on. They were still in the middle of opening up presents and normally Mom would never have let her put a DVD on. But she didn't object this time.

Annabel had made the DVD, and her voice narrated while she filmed favorite places they used to go, like the lake, the rec park, and the creemee stand. There were a few scenes at school, in the cafeteria and on the play-ground. Sarah and Kendall were in it too, talking into the camera and telling

Livvie how much they missed her. Sarah did a goofy imitation of Mr. Green, their gym teacher. All three girls were the same as always. The only thing different was that Livvie wasn't there with them. By the end, she was sobbing. Mom came over and put her arm around Livvie's shoulders.

"What a thoughtful gift," Grandma said. "You're lucky to have such good friends."

Livvie knew she meant well, but her words made Livvie cry harder. Mom sat beside her, rubbing her back and saying, "I know, Livvie, I know."

Livvie felt like screaming at her, "No, Mom, you don't know! How could you know? I didn't choose to come here like you did!" But she didn't want to start a big fight, especially on Christmas. So she made herself settle down and they got back to opening presents. She tried to act excited as she unwrapped packages, but her heart wasn't in it.

Afterwards, Mom made pancakes and bacon for brunch. Livvie wasn't hungry and picked at her food, blaming it on the big meal they had eaten the night before. Even though it was still morning, Grandma set out a dessert plate of the cutout sugar cookies they had made together, but Livvie just took a small one. She went back into the living room with it to watch the DVD again, clear-eyed this time, not wanting to miss any of the details.

As it was ending, Grandma came in and announced, "Livvie, there's one thing I want to do before I leave Aix."

"What, Grandma?" Livvie said, staring at the TV, thinking she was going to say she wanted to go to some museum or shop.

"I want to go down that big slide at the fun fair."

At this, Livvie looked up. She couldn't help but laugh at the thought of Grandma going down a giant plastic slide on a rubber mat.

Mom came in at the sound of laughter. "What's so funny? I'm dying to know."

"Get out of your apron," Grandma said. "We're all going down the big slide!"

The three of them threw on their jackets and headed over to the fun fair.

They practically ran along the sidewalk, like little kids. Grandma told a story about going on a roller coaster with Mom when she was a girl, and Mom laughed about being scared by the haunted house when they had all gone to Disneyworld three years ago. Livvie was just happy to be finally going on one of the rides, after walking past them and their red-cheeked occupants so many times.

They bought their tickets at the kiosk, selected a mat, and stepped onto the long ramp. Since it was still early, they were the only three on the ride. Grandma climbed up first. So Livvie and Mom could catch her if she slipped, she said. When they reached the top, they all sat down in a row, with Grandma in the middle. She grabbed both their hands as they pushed off, and they shrieked with laughter as they flew down. Grandma's new silk scarf fluttered behind them like a banner.

They went down four more times, until Mom and Grandma said they had had it, and they were all gasping for breath from laughing. The fresh air and the wind in Livvie's ears had worked—the day was finally feeling like Christmas. Not that it resembled Christmas back in Vermont very much, but it was special in its own way. In an Aix way. They walked back arm in arm to the apartment, their cheeks rosy and their hair windblown.

As Mom opened the door, the phone was ringing. Livvie dashed in to pick it up and, as she had been hoping, it was Dad.

"Merry Christmas, Livvie!"

"Merry Christmas, Dad."

"How're you doing? I'm sorry we're not together today, Livbug."

"Me too."

"Did you get my present?"

"Yeah, it's so cute. It looks like Clover."

"Well, Clover misses you and I thought you might be missing him too." Dad paused, and Livvie waited for him to tell her his surprise. "Thanks for the scarf," he continued. "It's beautiful. It'll keep me warm here in Boston. With the wind, sometimes it feels colder than Vermont."

"It's from the market here."

"The market? Cool. Hey, I have a surprise for you. I asked your mom not to tell you."

"She didn't tell me. What is it?" Livvie held her breath.

"I hear you have a vacation coming up in February. So I thought I would take a week off and come over to see you. We could spend some time together in Paris."

"That sounds great, Dad," Livvie said quietly.

"Don't get too excited. You'll have to be my translator, you know, since I don't speak any French. I'll pay you in ice cream; how's that for a deal?"

"Okay, I guess."

Livvie's head was a jumble of mixed emotions. She was relieved to say goodbye and hand the phone over to Mom. Grandma looked up as Livvie walked past her into the bathroom and shut the door. She didn't need to go, but she wanted a little privacy to sort out her thoughts.

Sitting down on the edge of the tub, she squeezed her eyes shut. How stupid of her to think they were getting back together. Although deep down she hadn't really believed they would. She ought to be happy that at least Dad was coming to visit. And she was. But she was a little nervous about it too. It also bothered her the way Dad had said "your mom." He never used to say that; it had always been "Mom." Livvie pictured him walking alone through the Boston Public Garden, near the pond with the swan boats. She imagined the pond frozen and an icy wind whipping through the empty park.

But then she pictured him with the scarf she had given him wrapped snugly around his neck. His hand was clutching the scarf and he was breathing through it to keep warm.

Livvie had bought the scarf from an old woman at the market. She had proudly described her flock of sheep that provided wool for her hand-knitted scarves. Mom had admired all the colors and patterns while Livvie took a long time deciding which one to get. When she had finally picked out a blue and green one and told the woman it was a gift for her father, the woman had said, "You're a good daughter."

Mom had said, "You're right, she is."

Livvie had smiled and thanked the woman, but was puzzled afterwards by her comment. How could that woman tell she was a good daughter? She had just met Livvie. Then she remembered that daughter and girl were the same word in French, fille, so maybe the woman had simply meant she was a good girl.

Chapter 17

The night before school started up again, Livvie dreamed for the first time in French. She and Malika were sitting on a bench talking, only it wasn't the bench at school. It was somewhere else, out in nature, with lots of green grass and trees around. Livvie couldn't remember what they were saying, but she woke up smiling.

As she left for school, she slung her new Chipie bag over her shoulder, patting it to make sure the book Malika had given her was inside. During vacation Livvie had tried to read it. It was called *Le Petit Prince*, and Livvie could understand most of it, even though it was kind of a complicated fantasy. Livvie loved fantasies, but this one was especially sad and the main character, the little prince, seemed lonely. It had a few funny parts too though. She hoped Malika had tried to read the book she had given her—*Ella Enchanted*, one of her all-time favorites.

At recess they huddled together on the bench to keep warm in the January chill.

"My dad had to help me with your book because I don't know enough English yet," Malika said.

"Did you tell him it was from me?"

Malika looked at the ground and Livvie immediately wished she hadn't asked. "He thought it was a school assignment," Malika said quietly.

"It's okay." Livvie hadn't told Mom that Malika had given her a book either.

"But I do like the book, Olivia."

"You can call me Livvie. It's what my family and friends usually call me."

"Okay, Livvie." She looked up.

"Do you have a shortened version of your name?" Livvie asked, unsure of what the word for nickname was in French.

"No. Everybody just calls me Malika."

"How about Lika? Can I call you Lika?"

"Oui, you can call me Lika." She smiled and her big, dark eyes shined like wishing stones.

As Livvie was leaving school that day, Nicole came up to her and handed her an envelope.

"It's a party," she said, "for my birthday."

"Merci," Livvie said, taking the envelope.

"I hope you can come. Nice bag, by the way." Nicole turned to join Sylvie and Pilar, who gave Livvie a little wave.

As Livvie walked toward her apartment, she slid the envelope open. Sure enough, it was an invitation, with a giant cake on the front. Inside was all the usual information—date, time, location—in pink calligraphy. The cold wind nearly pulled it out of her hand as she walked the rest of the way home.

Inside the apartment, Livvie dropped the invitation on the dining room table and went into her bedroom to start her homework. An hour later, when Mom stepped through the door, she immediately spotted the pink envelope on the table and picked it up.

"Livvie, how exciting! It'll be so much fun. And you'll get to know a whole new group of girls. She probably has a nice circle of friends, doesn't she?"

"Yeah, she has a circle. But I'm not sure they're my type."

"What do you mean, 'not your type'?"

"I don't know. They're all gorgeous, and popular, and always seem perfect."

"What's wrong with being attractive and smart and well-liked? You're all three of those things. You're probably just a little nervous because it's your first social event here. You'll have a fabulous time, you'll see."

"I'm not sure I want to go."

"Of course you're going to go. Don't be ridiculous. If you don't accept her invitation, you might not get any more." Mom spoke with such certainty that Livvie didn't dare object.

Chapter 18

The party was a week later at the bowling alley. Mom walked over with Livvie because it was all the way on the other side of town. As they started down Cours Mirabeau, Livvie looked around for the mime but he was nowhere to be seen. Not even his box. In fact, Livvie hadn't seen him since Christmas Eve and she was beginning to worry.

"Where do you think the mime is?" Livvie asked as they passed by the café near his usual spot.

"You mean that guy in the silver face paint?"

"Yeah, I haven't seen him around in a while."

"Maybe he went on to another town. Street performers move around a lot. There aren't as many tourists here in Aix this time of year so he probably moved on to Marseille or Paris."

"Moved on? Do you think he'll come back?" Livvie grabbed Mom's arm.

"Liv, I have no idea. Why are you so interested in him?"

"I don't know. I guess I got used to seeing him here."

"If he doesn't come back, I'm sure there'll be three or four to take his place once spring comes and it's tourist season again. But today, you have a party to go to. Your first French party! That's pretty exciting, don't you think?" Mom shook her arm free and put it around Livvie's shoulder.

"Yeah, I guess. But she probably only invited me so the teams would be even."

"Don't be silly."

"It also seems weird that the party's at a bowling alley. Nicole doesn't seem like the bowling type."

"Maybe bowling is popular here. You'll get to know all sorts of things about French 'tweens."

When they arrived at the bowling alley and stepped inside the large, dimly lit space, row after row of shiny lanes unfolded before them like any bowling alley back home. This one had a nicer eating area, though, called the Café de Bowling. Nicole was easy to spot in there, standing around talking with some other girls. Her mother was chatting with another well-dressed woman. A few of the tables had been pushed together and covered with a hot pink tablecloth. Pink balloons bumped the low ceiling overhead.

As Livvie and Mom walked through the café entrance, the girls all turned around and looked at them. Nicole stepped forward and gave Livvie a kiss on each cheek. Her mother did the same and exclaimed, "Olivia, I'm so glad you could come."

She greeted Mom and within seconds they were chatting like old friends. Nicole turned back to her conversation with the other girls. Livvie recognized them from school, from the circle on the playground, but didn't know their names. She stood there for a few minutes feeling awkward. Coming here was a mistake, she could tell already. She wished Lika had been invited, but she knew it wasn't likely and she hadn't asked Lika if she was going. Livvie had never seen any of the Chipies talking to Lika. Not that they were ever mean to her. They just didn't seem interested in getting to know her.

Livvie realized she was still holding Nicole's gift and debated whether she should hand it to her now and interrupt her, or set it on the table with the other gifts. She went with the easier choice and set it on the table. It was a small purse, and it looked tiny compared to the other packages. At least it had the Chipie label on it.

A few other girls streamed in, including Sylvie and Pilar who arrived together. Mom came over to say goodbye and whispered, "Mingle, sweetie, mingle. Don't be shy."

"Okay, Mom." Livvie glared at her, but turned to Sylvie and Pilar and said, "Salut."

"Salut," they said in unison.

"I like your boots," Sylvie said.

"Merci, yours are nice too," Livvie said, surprised by how easily she responded in French.

"I wish we didn't have to wear those ugly bowling shoes. Do you think they'll make us?" Pilar said, grimacing.

"I hope not. Do you go bowling a lot?" Livvie asked.

"Not so much," Sylvie laughed. "Only at birthday parties."

"How about you?" Pilar asked.

"No, not very much. I used to go sometimes with my family back in the US."

"Hopefully the three of us will be on the same team, so we won't embarrass ourselves too much," Sylvie said.

By now all the guests had arrived. Eight girls in all. A man from the bowling alley went through the rules as he handed out shoes. He spoke quickly and with such a different accent that Livvie couldn't understand much of what he said, but she followed what the other girls did. After he led them to their lanes, Nicole announced that she had divided the girls up into two teams. Livvie would be with Sylvie and Pilar, and another petite, red-haired girl named Amandine whom Livvie recognized from recess.

They played two games, and a little way into the first one Livvie realized she was actually having fun. She was never much into bowling, but something about the familiar weight of the ball in her hands made her relax. And the balls thwacked as they hit the pins the same way they did back home. The girls cheered each other on, tried out some of the techniques the man had demonstrated, and laughed at their bad throws. Pilar was the best on their team, with the accuracy and grace of a natural athlete. Livvie wasn't bad either. Sylvie was the worst, but she was a good sport about it, joking that she was the mascot. She redid her ponytail high on top of her head and held it up in two long pieces like ears. She jumped around like some kind of crazy rabbit and they all cracked up.

Each team ended up winning a game. They gave each other high fives, and Nicole announced that they all needed to line up to receive their prize of a pink lip gloss. Livvie was the only one who seemed to find this annoying. But while they were waiting, Sylvie whispered to Livvie, "I can't stand how Nicole always wants to be in charge."

When it was time for cake, Nicole's mom lit the candles, and the other woman who was there at the beginning poured the drinks. Nicole called her Tante Charlotte so Livvie figured she must be Nicole's aunt. There wasn't a dad around. Maybe her parents were split up too.

At the table, Livvie had taken a seat beside Sylvie. When the cake was served, a towering pink and yellow confection, Sylvie slid the candy decorations off of her slice and offered them to Livvie. The cake was extremely sweet and Livvie wasn't hungry, but she thanked Sylvie and took them anyway.

After that it was time for presents. Nicole examined the pile of gifts on the table, and selected from them in a particular order. She chose one from a girl named Gabrielle first. Livvie had seen her at recess hanging around with Nicole's group. She was hard to miss since she was really tall and thin. She was even taller than Livvie, which was unusual for a French girl. Her blond hair was cut like Mom's, short in the back but falling longer to her chin. And she had enormous, brown eyes. She looked so chic, like some kind of model.

Gabrielle's present was huge. Nicole held it on her lap and carefully unwrapped it. The paper fell away to reveal a large, white linen throw pillow with Nicole's name embroidered in ornate, pink script. What a grown-up gift. It was more like the kind of thing someone would give Mom. Nicole ran her hand over the script, admiring it, then squeezed the pillow to her chest. Gabrielle smiled and dipped her chin so her hair slid in front of her face.

Nicole opened some other presents, carefully choosing, until there were two left. Livvie's and Sylvie's. She selected Livvie's first. When she lifted the purse out of its box, she cried, "Maman, it's the purse I wanted!" She draped it over her shoulder and gushed, "Merci, Olivia."

Livvie let her breath out, relieved that she liked it. Even though Nicole was annoying, Livvie was glad she had included her. And she wasn't all that different from girls Livvie knew back home. Kendall could be kind of spoiled sometimes. And pretty bossy if they let her get away with it.

The other girls weren't so different either. They laughed about the same kinds of things Livvie and her friends would have laughed about. There were similar issues with playing favorites. And even though Livvie and her friends didn't wear expensive Chipie clothes back home, they all did wear a lot of Gap and Old Navy. These girls might have been more sophisticated than Livvie's friends in Vermont, but that was probably because Aix was a lot bigger than Hinesburg. And this was France after all, the land of style, as Mom said.

At school, these girls were in an exclusive clique, but Livvie wondered if that was how she and her friends had seemed to some of the other kids in her grade. They always did sit together at lunch and hang out together on the playground. They were nice enough to everybody, but they didn't exactly seek out other friends to be part of their group. Livvie remembered when that new girl Rachel had sat near them a few times and they hadn't made a big effort to include her in their conversation.

But why had Nicole invited Livvie and not Malika? She had to have noticed that Livvie and Malika were friends. Maybe they had had a big disagreement about something. Or maybe it had to do with Malika being a Muslim. Livvie decided she was going to mention something about Nicole to Lika at recess on Monday and see what she said.

Chapter 19

It was an unusually warm day for January, warm enough for Livvie and Lika to unzip their jackets as they walked over to their bench at recess. All morning Livvie had worried over asking Lika about the Chipies. They were in their usual cluster in the courtyard, talking and turning their faces like flowers to the sun. As Livvie sat down, Sylvie looked over at her and smiled. Livvie smiled back and waved. Sylvie waved back and then, to Livvie's surprise, she stepped away from the group and walked toward them.

"Salut, Olivia," Sylvie said. She glanced at Lika beside her and said, "Salut."

"Salut, Sylvie," Livvie answered. "Ca va?"

"Ca va bien. What a pretty day—I feel like going to the beach!"

They talked about the weather for a few minutes, until Sylvie headed back over to the group, her ponytail swinging behind her. Lika hadn't said anything during the whole conversation. She had just sat there shrunken into herself like she wanted to be smaller, watching her feet make circles in the gravel. Livvie wished she had tried to include her somehow. But at least Sylvie coming over made it easier to bring up the topic of the Chipies.

"Do you know Sylvie?" Livvie asked.

"No, not very well. She's part of Nicole's group."

"Yeah, but she's pretty nice. Nicole's not bad either, except she's a little bossy. Have you gone to school with them for a while?"

"Since I was seven."

"I'm surprised you don't know them better."

"Yeah, they have their own group, you know." She looked down at her feet again, this time pushing some gravel into a small pile.

Livvie watched the pile get bigger until Lika gently squashed it with her foot. Livvie wasn't sure what else to say. Lika started to make another pile so Livvie changed the subject.

"Guess what, Lika. I'm going to Paris during the vacation. My dad's coming over to visit and I'm so excited!"

"That's great, Livvie."

"It'll be my first visit to Paris. Except for a short stop on our way over. But that doesn't count because I was only in the airport. Have you ever been there?"

"Oui, a few times. I have some relatives there. It's a beautiful city." Lika's feet had stilled, but she kept her head down.

"I can't wait. My mom says she thinks it's the most beautiful city in the world. She's talked about it my whole life. I want to go all the way up to the top of the Eiffel Tower. Have you done that?"

"Non, I wanted to, but my maman is afraid of heights."

"That's too bad. I also want to try to find the mime. I was thinking he might have gone up to Paris for the winter."

"Maybe. He'll be back, though, in the spring. He always comes back in the spring." Lika finally looked up.

"He does?"

"Yeah. He goes away the same time every year, but he always comes back."

"I'm so glad! I really miss him."

"I miss him too," Lika said.

Livvie got into his Thinker pose, and Lika smiled. Livvie smiled too, for the rest of the day, since she knew she could count on the mime coming back.

Chapter 20

"Don't forget to pack your raincoat, Liv. And good walking shoes!" Mom called from her bedroom.

"D'accord," Livvie said, sliding her sneakers into the outside pocket of her suitcase. This was the first time she'd used her luggage since arriving in France six months before. When she was packing last time, she had tried to cram as much as she possibly could into the seemingly tiny space. Now, the suitcase's compartments yawned open on the bed as Livvie carefully folded and placed her clothes. She held up a Chipie sweater, debating about whether to bring that or her old, favorite Gap sweatshirt. The stuffed Clover Dad had given her sat on a pillow watching her.

"What do you think? Should I bring this?" Mom suddenly ducked her head in the doorway wearing a jaunty hat pulled low over one eye.

"Sure, if you want." Livvie shrugged.

Mom disappeared and was off in high gear, racing around the apartment pulling out all kinds of clothes. Livvie wasn't sure if her energy was from excitement about their trip, or if she was nervous about seeing Dad. She would just see him briefly though. After spending the first day with Livvie in Paris before Dad arrived, she would go on to a work conference in London and meet up with Livvie again at the end of the week. A week Livvie would be spending alone with Dad.

The next day Livvie and Mom boarded the TGV, a super-fast train, the same one they had taken on their way down to Aix six months before. As they retraced their path to Paris, speeding over the same bridges and through the same tunnels, Livvie wondered if Dad would think she had changed. If she was different in any way. Her reflection in the train's window, superimposed over the blurry countryside, looked pretty much the same as before. The same honey brown hair falling past her shoulders. The same blue eyes and broad cheeks. Unlike Mom, who looked completely different.

Livvie glanced over at her across the aisle. She was on her cell phone with someone from work, her chocolate brown hair falling to her chin. Her nails were polished pale pink with white tips, something called a French manicure. She had on those pointy, black shoes she wore all the time and a short, black trench coat—a big change from her Plain Jane look back in Vermont.

But maybe Livvie was more different on the inside. She could speak French now—that was new. Grandma had said she was brave, and part of her did feel brave for having survived going to school in a foreign country. But how else was she different? She knew she wasn't the same girl who had ridden the train down from Paris back in August, but she didn't know exactly why.

They arrived in Paris in the early afternoon and got right on the métro, the French subway, at the train station. Livvie had been on a subway a few times before, in New York and Boston, so this one didn't seem that special. But Mom was bursting.

"You're going to love it, Livvie! I remember the first time I saw Paris when I came here as a student. I couldn't believe human beings had created such a place. Its beauty took my breath away. And every time I've been back, I feel the same way."

Livvie nodded and tried to act excited, but she found it hard to believe a city could be so amazing. New York and Boston were both fun to visit, but she would never call them breath-taking.

They stepped off the subway and climbed the well-worn stairs up to the street, Livvie struggling with her luggage to keep up with Mom. When they surfaced, they were standing beside the Seine, the river dividing Paris into the Right and Left Bank. They were on the Left Bank and across from them on an island in the middle of the river, Notre Dame shimmered like a giant, sculpted sand castle.

Livvie had seen Notre Dame before in photos but in person, with its intricate carvings and graceful flying buttresses, it was something else altogether. It soared above the surrounding buildings with its arching supports defying gravity. Livvie's breath caught in her throat. She looked to the left across the Seine to another building with pointed turrets.

Mom followed her gaze and cried, "That's the Conciergerie—a Medieval palace! Isn't it magnificent? And the bridges, look at the bridges—they're works of art. And over there, that other little island is called Île St-Louis. It's one of my favorite parts of Paris. Oh, Livvie, isn't it incredible?"

She was right. It was incredible. Livvie felt like she was standing inside a painting. But it was a real, living, breathing city, with cars going by and people pushing past them on the sidewalk. "It is amazing, Mom."

They stood there admiring the view for a few more minutes, while people stepped around their luggage.

"Come on, Liv," Mom finally said. "The hotel's a few blocks from here over by the Jardin du Luxembourg. We can unpack and go get a bite to eat at a crêperie. I just get to be here with you for one day, and I don't want to waste any time."

It was more than a few blocks of hauling their luggage along the bumpy sidewalk, but Livvie didn't mind. They were in the part of Paris known as the Latin Quarter, where the Sorbonne is located. Mom had studied at that university when she was in college and, as they walked along, she pointed out places she remembered. Artsy cafés and little hidden away streets. Fountains and quiet gardens filled with weathered sculpture. Livvie couldn't recall when Mom had ever been this excited. This alive.

After they checked in to their hotel, they headed back out into the streets of Paris. They bought some crêpes from a street vendor, their gooey chocolate oozing out with every bite. Then, over the next twenty-four hours, Mom took Livvie on a whirlwind tour of her favorite places. They stopped only to sleep after a late night boat ride on the Seine and woke up early to have a croissant and chocolat chaud at one of the lively cafés in the neighborhood.

Mom kept Livvie so busy that she almost forgot she would be seeing Dad. Part of her had been trying not to think about it too much. Whenever she did, her insides started belly dancing from nerves or excitement, she wasn't sure which.

Mom had arranged for Dad to meet them at the hotel later that morning because he'd be staying there with Livvie while Mom was in London. As the time of his arrival got closer, Mom kept looking at her watch and Livvie could smell cigarette smoke on her clothes after she went down to the lobby to check on him. Livvie lay on one of the beds and tried to read, but her eyes skimmed the same paragraph over and over. Finally, an hour after he was due, someone knocked on the door. Mom stopped flipping through her magazine and looked up, frozen. Livvie jumped off the bed and flung open the door.

It was Dad. He stood there, his luggage at his feet, with a boyish expression on his face. Livvie threw her arms around him, and he leaned down and picked her up in one of his big bear hugs. Tears filled Livvie's eyes as she breathed in his smell.

"Hey, Livbug!" he said. "It's great to see you!"

Livvie kept on hugging him until he laughed and his shoulders relaxed.

"Hi, Jeff," Mom said from behind them.

"Hey there," Dad said, putting Livvie down. "New haircut. That looks good on you."

"Thanks." Mom brushed her hair back from her face. "How was the flight?"

"Long. But it's great to be here. Nice room."

"Yeah, you should be comfortable here. Did the desk give you another key?"

Livvie stared at them as they talked awkwardly about hotel details. Then

Mom picked up her bag. "Have fun, Liv," she said with a kiss. She gave Dad a wave saying, "I'll see you Saturday."

The door closed and Dad turned to Livvie. She resisted the urge to shake her head to clear it, like she was waking up from a bizarre dream.

"Liv, you look great. You've gotten taller, or is it those French fashions making you look that way?"

"I don't know, maybe I've grown a little. You look the same."

"I am the same. I'm your same old Dad. A little tired from the jetlag, but nothing some ice cream won't cure. How about if I unpack and we go for a walk around the neighborhood? You don't mind being the navigator and translator, do you, because I don't speak a word of French. Your mom says you're practically fluent already."

"Yeah, it's a lot easier now."

"That's good. It must have been impossible at first. When your mother came up with this idea to bring you over here with her, I thought she was out of her mind. But you know how she is when she gets an idea in her head."

This was weird too, Dad talking about Mom that way. Livvie changed the subject. "Will you go up the Eiffel Tower with me, Dad?"

"Sure, Livbug, whatever you want to do. We've got five days in Paris, and your wish is my command."

Livvie expected the five days to fly by, but they didn't. It was fun, but when Dad said she would be the navigator and translator, he meant it. He didn't even try to speak French, not even bonjour or merci. And he didn't have a lot of patience with the waiters and taxi drivers who couldn't speak English. They made it up to the top of the Eiffel Tower, though, and Dad held her hand when she felt dizzy on the elevator. They also went to the top of the Arc de Triomphe, which stands at one end of the famous boulevard, the Champs-Elysées. Cars circled below them as they looked out over the city.

"Isn't it beautiful, Dad?"

"It's nice. All the gray buildings are a little dreary though. I don't get why it's called the City of Light, with all these gray buildings."

"Mom says it's because Paris is a center of knowledge and culture. Since way back in the time of the Enlightenment. Most people now think it's because of all the buildings being lit up at night with thousands of lights."

"Now that I'd like to see. We'll have to take a tour around the city after dinner."

So that night, they snuggled together in the back of a taxi and admired all the twinkling white lights and gleaming buildings. Livvie had seen a lot of them already when she and Mom had gone on the boat ride, but she didn't mention this to Dad. Cuddled next to him with his arm around her shoulder, laughing at the taxi driver's wild turns, she closed her eyes and they were back in Vermont. Mom was in the front seat with the driver, and the three of them were happy and together in the warm closeness of a car.

"Tired?" Dad asked, rubbing her shoulder. "Maybe we should have the cabbie swing us back up to the room. Could you ask him?"

Livvie opened her eyes and leaned forward, avoiding looking at the empty passenger seat in front. She quietly asked the driver to take them back to the hotel.

The next morning they slept in, and over breakfast Dad suggested they try bungee jumping on the trampolines set up in front of the Louvre. They were supposed to be for kids, but Dad climbed right up beside Livvie and they both bounced as high as they could. Dad even tried to do some flips, which made Livvie laugh so hard she almost cried.

His last night in Paris, Dad made a big deal of surprising Livvie by taking her out to dinner at Joe Allen, an American restaurant. He said he thought she was probably desperately missing American food. She wasn't, but played along. Surrounded by American posters and memorabilia, they ordered Buffalo wings and guacamole for appetizers, followed by a platter of barbecued ribs with corn on the cob and cole slaw. The food was like a backyard cookout on a summer holiday, but it tasted oddly unfamiliar to Livvie. And not nearly as good as most of the French food she'd gotten used to eating.

Over dinner she asked Dad if he liked living in Boston.

"Yeah, it's okay. As far as cities go. But I'm a country boy at heart. I miss hiking. And birdwatching."

"Do you think you'll move back to Vermont?"

"I don't know. I have this new job now at a bigger radio station. So I'm managing more people. There are a lot more opportunities for me there."

"Do you like the DJs there?"

"Yeah, they're great. You met one of them. Do you remember Becky? Becky Catrell? She was up in Vermont for a year. Thought she wanted a change from the city. But she decided to go back to her old job."

"I remember her." She had stopped by the house one day on her bike. She was friendly and pretty with a big smile and a tattoo of a crescent moon on her ankle. She had chatted with Dad for a while in the yard. Dad had made her some iced tea. When he talked about her in the restaurant, he kept clearing his throat.

"Yeah, Becky helped me get the job. I kind of wanted a change. And, well, she's nice. You'd like her." They gnawed on their corn for a few minutes in silence. "You wouldn't believe Clover. She's a real city cat now. She goes racing through the stairwell in my apartment building like she owns it."

"She probably misses running around in the fields."

"Yeah, you're probably right. But she still catches plenty of mice." Dad licked some barbecue sauce off his fingers. "So how's your mom doing? Is she happy here in France finally?"

"Yeah, I guess," Livvie said. She took a sip of her root beer as other questions rose to her lips: Wasn't Mom happy in Vermont? If not, why? And why would Dad care whether she liked Becky Catrell? But before she could say anything, the English-speaking waiter stopped by their table and Dad got into a conversation with him about Boston and baseball, and the questions were left unspoken.

Chapter 21

Dad was brushing his teeth and Livvie was packing up her suitcase when Mom quietly knocked on the door and called out, "Livvie? Jeff?"

Her key clicked in the lock and the door opened.

Livvie surprised both Mom and herself when she cried "Mommy!" and ran over to give her a big kiss.

"Livvie! I missed you too!" Mom said laughing.

Dad stepped out of the bathroom, toothbrush in hand, his hair still damp from a shower.

"Hi, Jeff."

"Hi, Diane. How was London?"

"Very nice. But not as nice as Paris. Did you two have fun?"

"Did we have fun? We had an awesome time, didn't we, Liv?"

"Yeah, it was great." Livvie zipped her suitcase shut and sat down on the bed.

Dad puttered around the room gathering up his things, while Mom sat in a chair leafing through a Paris guidebook. During that brief time when the three of them were all together in the room, maybe twenty minutes, Livvie tried to focus on their simple nearness to her. Then Dad said his goodbyes, gave her a gigantic bear hug, and he was gone.

Mom flopped down on the bed beside Livvie and said, "So how'd it go?"

"We had a good time."

"How did he like Paris?"

"Ummm … not as much as you and I do."

"I'm not surprised. He's never been a big fan of France. That's his misfortune, isn't it? How's he's doing?"

"Okay, I guess."

"Did he mention anything about ... never mind. I shouldn't be probing you. We have one more afternoon in Paris. We need to live it up. How about if we go over to the Rodin Museum? He's that famous sculptor who did The Thinker."

"Yeah, that sounds good."

On the way over to the museum, Livvie hoped she would finally see the mime. She had expected to have spotted him somewhere in Paris by now. At most of the main tourist sites she had visited, there were always several mimes around. But not her mime—or their mime, she corrected herself, re-membering Lika.

He wasn't at the Rodin Museum either. But seeing the real sculpture of The Thinker almost made up for it. The sculpture was outside in the muse-um's orderly garden, its bronze surface gleaming in the misty air. Livvie gazed up at it, at the rough base on which the man sat, at his lifelike muscles. Water droplets trickled down his curved back. She walked around to the front and looked up at his face. His expression was pensive, mysterious, almost peace-ful. It looked exactly like the pose the mime did. She couldn't wait to tell Lika she had seen it.

On the train ride back to Aix, Livvie pulled a miniature Eiffel Tower out of her bag. She had bought it for Lika. The metal felt solid and cool in her hand. Dad had bought her a tiny, silver one for her charm bracelet at the same shop, and it dangled on her wrist next to Lika's gift. Sometimes the two of them touched and made a humming sound from the vibrations of the train thundering south.

They arrived back in Aix at dusk, and Mom suggested they walk the short distance to their apartment. Wandering up Cours Mirabeau and through the narrow streets, past familiar fountains and cafés and splashes of graffiti, a thought formed in Livvie's mind—it was good to be back home. The thought startled her and she argued with herself that, no, home was back in Vermont. But the thought wouldn't let go.

They passed by their boulangerie, its warm glow spilling out onto the sidewalk. Madame looked up from behind the counter and waved as they walked by. Even the dog poop on the sidewalks wasn't so bad anymore. She stepped around it automatically.

They reached their building, with its signature smiley face on the door. Livvie smiled back at it and entered the stairwell. The sound of Monsieur Cantini's violin floated in the air, along with the smell of garlic and herbs from the Durands' dinner preparations. Something delicious was always wafting out of their apartment around this time. Livvie slipped off her shoes without even thinking. As they climbed the stairs, she realized she was no longer arguing with herself. This was her home now.

Mom must have been feeling it too. When she opened the door to their apartment, she said, "Home sweet home." A few months ago that comment would have bothered Livvie. But now she repeated it as she rolled her luggage into her bedroom. A rosy light was slanting in through her windows so she walked over and looked out. The sky was gorgeous, a watercolor wash of orange and red. Sainte Victoire hovered there in the middle of it all, a deep pink. There was a glow around it like a halo, interrupted only by the outline of that cross at the top.

Chapter 22

The miniature Eiffel Tower made the pocket of Livvie's Chipie school-bag bulge out in an odd way. She tried moving it around so it wasn't too obvious, but it didn't fit anywhere else. So she put her hand over the bump and hoped Mom didn't ask her about it when she kissed her goodbye. Mom was in a rush that morning and didn't notice.

On the walk over to school, Livvie wondered what she was worried about. Why hadn't she mentioned Lika to Mom? Why would she not want to tell Mom she had gotten her a present from their trip to Paris? Livvie had never heard Mom say anything negative about Muslims, and she didn't think of Mom as a prejudiced person. But for some reason she had a hunch Mom wouldn't be overjoyed about her friendship with Lika. Mom was much more interested in Livvie being friends with someone like Nicole. Livvie wondered if Lika's parents felt the same way.

During recess, Livvie gave the Eiffel Tower to Lika.

"Merci, I love it," Lika said, smiling. "I'll keep it on my desk at home."

Her smile faded.

"What's the matter?" Livvie asked.

"Oh, nothing. I was just thinking about my parents. They might ask where I got it."

"You don't want to tell them it's from a friend at school?"

"Well … they'll probably want to know who the friend is."

Livvie took a deep breath, and asked, "Is it because I'm American?"

Lika hesitated, looking down. "You know, with everything that's gone on, and what your country has been doing in Muslim countries … .My parents are not big fans of the US and how your country has been treating Muslims.

It's not about you. It's that … they might not understand." She set the Eiffel Tower on the bench between them.

"It's okay. I think I know what you mean. You could always say it's from a French friend."

"Non, I don't want to lie to them. Besides, they know I don't have any good friends at school."

"Do you have other friends you hang out with?"

"I have friends from the mosque, and lots of cousins. They all go to school in Marseille." Lika picked the Eiffel Tower up again and slowly traced its outline with her finger. "We moved to Aix when I was seven. Papa said it would be safer and I'd get a better education. But they don't seem to want me to be friends with anyone. Sometimes I wonder why they decided to move here at all. I know they have more money than most of my relatives, but they could have stayed in Marseille. They seem a lot more comfortable there."

As she spoke, Lika's voice became more and more forceful. Her eyes looked straight into Livvie's as she continued. "Once, a few years ago, I got an invitation to Sylvie's birthday party. I think she may have invited the whole class, but still I was excited to go. But Maman said I couldn't. She said it was because she didn't know Sylvie's family. It's not fair! Maman and Papa don't understand anything about my life!"

"Neither do my mom and dad. They don't listen to me half the time. Mom thinks she always knows what's best for me, so a lot of the time it's easier to not say anything at all."

"Does your mother know about me?"

Livvie looked down and said, "Non, I haven't told her. It's not that she has anything against Muslims but … I don't know. I don't know what she'd think. But it shouldn't matter at all. I mean, you're my friend, and I like hanging out with you. It shouldn't matter what your religion is!"

"You're right," Lika said. "It shouldn't matter. Thank you for the Eiffel Tower, Livvie. I'm going to bring it home and put it on my desk."

Later that day, Livvie went over the conversation with Lika in her head. She was glad they had finally talked openly about their parents. But something about the conversation bothered her—what Lika had said about how the US was treating Muslims. She hadn't said it in an accusing way, more as a matter of fact. Even though Livvie didn't want to admit it, she knew what Lika was talking about. She had read little bits of news on the Internet and had seen headlines in the French newspapers. Livvie hadn't wanted to think about it, so she had tried to push it out of her head. But she knew it was happening. How could Lika's family not be upset by what the US was doing? Livvie had never felt ashamed to be American before, but a small part of her felt that way now.

While Livvie was getting ready for bed that night, Mom came into her room with a pile of clean laundry. The conversation was still on Livvie's mind so she decided to bring it up. "Mom, what do you think about the US and what's going on in the Middle East?"

"It's a real mess over there. Such a sad situation. I hope it settles down soon. Why do you ask? Did someone say something to you at school?" She separated the laundry into piles, Livvie's and hers.

"Sort of. I mean, it doesn't seem as if the US is always doing the right thing."

"I don't know if we'll ever know the truth about it all. It's a complicated situation. And the French don't always agree with our policies so I'm not surprised it's come up at school. But I think we're united on opposing terrorists, which is the main issue." Mom handed her a pair of pajamas. They were stiff and cold from being outside on the drying rack.

"Who are these terrorists?"

"They're the people who flew the planes into the World Trade Center and have blown up other buildings and trains full of innocent people. Like in Spain and London and other parts of the world. They're usually Muslim extremists, and they're trying to destroy our way of life."

"What are extremists?" Livvie shivered as she slipped on the pajamas.

"They're fanatics, radicals. They often use violence to make themselves heard. Of course not all Muslims are extremists. But unfortunately there are those few who cause trouble. France has had to deal with it too." Mom folded the laundry into two neat stacks as she continued, "You probably noticed the guys with the machine guns at the Eiffel Tower. And the clear trash containers on the streets of Paris—that's to keep people from putting bombs in them. Back in the 1990s they had a lot of problems with terrorists, especially Algerians, you know, from North Africa."

"I wonder how the other Muslims feel about it though, the ones who aren't extremists. If they feel like people who aren't Muslim think they're the enemy or something."

"That's a big question, Livvie. I guess you'd have to ask them." Mom scooped up her stack of laundry.

"Do you know any Muslims?"

"Not personally. A few of them work in my office, and I have nothing against them. I just don't know them. So I don't think I'm about to go up and ask them how they feel about terrorism. Besides, they're different from us."

"Well, it could be kind of interesting to get to know them and find out how they feel about things. You might become friends with them. Maybe they're not so different after all."

"Yeah, I suppose." Mom walked toward the door and then turned and said, "Hey, speaking of friends from work, I'm going out for coffee tomorrow with someone from the office. His name's Jean-Pierre. So I'll be a little late getting home. You can finish up your homework and we'll have dinner when I get back, d'accord?"

"Sure, no problem. Is it a date, Mom?"

"No, it's only coffee. But I wouldn't mind if it led to a date. He's cute, and très français."

"Oh là là," Livvie said teasing, but deep down she wasn't sure what she thought about Mom going out on a date.

Chapter 23

"Olivia! We're heading down to Cours Mirabeau for some glace. Want to come?" Nicole called from across the street. She was walking arm in arm with Gabrielle, that tall, perfect girl from her party. Pilar and Sylvie followed arm in arm behind them.

"Um, sure." Livvie waited for a cluster of motorbikes to hum by before crossing the street.

Sylvie held out her other arm and slipped it into Livvie's. "Ca va?"

"Ca va bien. And you?"

"Ca va bien."

As they walked under the big chestnut tree on the corner, some of its flower petals fluttered down on them. It was March and spring had arrived in Aix, bringing with it warm breezes, the return of that brilliant Mediterranean sun, and flowering trees everywhere. Some of the delicate, white petals brightened the sidewalk and reminded Livvie that in Vermont it was still winter. Snow was probably still blanketing the ground. Just last week, Annabel had sent a picture of her and Kendall skiing at Sugarbush. Livvie was never much of a skier, and even though she still missed her Vermont friends, she didn't miss the long, gray winter.

"There's my house, Olivia," Nicole said, bringing Livvie back to Aix. She was pointing to a three-story building, similar to the one Livvie lived in, but much bigger and fancier. The yellow stone was sculpted into elegant garlands and curlicues, and the windows were decorated with elaborate iron grillework. There was some kind of official-looking crest above the double front doors. The doors themselves were massive and at the center of each was a big, brass knocker in the shape of a lion's head. There was no graffiti on her building.

"Which floor are you on?" Livvie looked up at the balcony on third floor.

"We live on the top two, and that's Maman's shop on the ground floor."

She was referring to a très chic woman's clothing store that Mom had walked by a million times drooling. All of the clothes were by the of-the-moment designers in France. Mom had joked she could only afford to buy their scented soap.

"Does your mom work there?" Livvie asked.

"Yeah. A lot. Especially now since she and Papa split up. She's afraid she might lose the shop. She isn't there today though. She's with Grand-mère."

So Nicole's parents were divorced as Livvie had suspected. And she wasn't surprised Nicole lived in such an upscale building, but she was surprised it was so close to her own apartment.

"Do you live nearby too?" Livvie asked Sylvie.

"Not far. We have a little apartment over by the Cathédrale."

"And she has a house down on the coast, lucky girl." Pilar tugged on Sylvie's elbow, making Livvie stumble a little too.

"Yeah, but not as lucky as you, with those hot twin brothers!" Sylvie tugged back. "Olivia can have Juan if I get Carlo. You'll have to come over to Pilar's pool this summer, Olivia. You won't believe these guys. Pilar's mom is Spanish and they all have the same gorgeous, black curls."

"Don't be such a groupie, Sylvie." Nicole glanced back, looking at Livvie. "Where should we go? The usual?"

"Sure," Gabrielle agreed. "Le Bastide has the best glace."

They had reached the Cours by now and were heading down to Le Bastide. Livvie knew the café because it was the one right beside the mime's old spot. He still hadn't come back and lately Livvie had been afraid that maybe he never would. But, as they got closer—could it be true?— his white box was peeking out from behind a tree. And there he was standing on his box, in his same white clothing and silver paint!

Livvie grabbed Sylvie's arm and cried, "He's back!"

"Who's back?" Sylvie asked.

"The mime! He's been gone all winter, but now he's back!" Livvie practically pulled Sylvie down the sidewalk, pushing ahead of Nicole and Gabrielle.

"Do you know him?" Sylvie was staring at Livvie as they stumbled down the sidewalk.

"Is he a friend of yours?" Nicole's thick eyebrows came together to form a V.

"No, I just think he's cool."

By now they were right in front of the mime. He stood with his left arm outstretched and had a stern expression on his face, as if he had been caught in a heated conversation. He was perfectly still, his silver paint shimmering in the sun. Suddenly he smiled, reached his hand up as if to take off a top hat, and did an exaggerated bow. When he looked up, his eyes stopped on Livvie. His warm, brown eyes, the color of the café au lait Mom had each morning. He blew kisses to each of them, as Livvie was pulled away by the elbow by Sylvie, who was being pulled by Pilar.

"No, thank you," said Pilar. "I don't think I want to kiss him."

"No way." Gabrielle scrunched up her pointy, little nose.

"Are you sure you don't know him, Olivia?" Nicole asked, choosing a table in the outdoor seating area. "He looked at you like he knew you."

"No, I don't know him at all. I just like to watch him."

"I'd stay away from him," Nicole said. "A lot of those street performers are homeless. He might try to steal from you, or worse."

"He's been coming here for years, Nicole." Sylvie rolled her eyes. "He seems pretty harmless to me."

"Yeah, but you never know." Pilar fiddled with her napkin. "You Americans are much more open than the French, Olivia. You know, like how you're friends with that Muslim girl in our class."

Livvie froze. She swallowed and said, "You mean Malika? She's really nice."

"She may be nice, but they're different from us, Olivia. Do you know her mother wears a headscarf?" Nicole fluffed out her hair. "I wonder if her parents are going to force her to wear one, or maybe even send her back to Algeria to get married when she's sixteen."

Gabrielle nodded, but no one said anything else. They all looked at Livvie, waiting for her response. Livvie sat there staring at the black and white checkered tablecloth, the squares starkly contrasting against each other. But where they touched, there was a faint gray edge.

"I like Malika," Livvie finally said. "I've gotten to know her and we actually have a lot in common." More than you and I, Nicole, Livvie wanted to add but didn't.

"She's definitely smart," Sylvie said. "I sat near her last year and she was always getting high grades on everything."

"Yeah, well, no one said terrorists are stupid," Nicole said, her pink glossed lips carefully forming each word.

"Terrorist! Malika's not a terrorist!" Livvie pushed her chair back at the same time. It scraped the floor, and the people at the table beside them gave her a look.

"Yeah, Nicole, that's a little ridiculous, don't you think?" Sylvie said.

"I'm not saying Malika's a terrorist," Nicole's pink lips continued. "All I'm saying is you don't know anything about her family, Olivia. Or what they might be involved in. So again, you need to be careful."

"We don't want to see you getting into a bad situation, because you're not as familiar with the French culture, that's all," Pilar chimed in.

"What can I get for you, Mesdemoiselles?" the waiter asked, directing their attention toward ordering ice cream. Livvie was grateful for the interruption, but the whole conversation, from the mime to Malika, left her with no appetite. How could Nicole think Malika's parents are terrorists! Just because of their religion! And what about Pilar? With her dark coloring and strong features, she and Lika could be sisters, two beautiful sisters. But because Lika was Muslim she was automatically an outsider. Different. Not to be trusted.

When the waiter left, Pilar started talking about her pool again. How she always had a pool party sometime during the summer, and how this year Livvie would definitely be invited. Livvie smiled and nodded, but her thoughts were miles away—with Annabel and Kendall on that pristine mountain in Vermont, far from this place and these girls. They would understand, wouldn't they? Or would they judge Lika in the same way the Chipies did? Livvie remembered how closed their circle was to other kids, how they would sometimes even make fun of kids who were different in some way. Like the girl whose parents were refugees from Cambodia—she couldn't even remember her name now—and Dylan, that boy who stuttered. They had never bothered to get to know them. She had never bothered to get to know them. She was as bad as these girls.

Soon the silver dishes arrived with their smooth, creamy balls of vanilla. Livvie still wasn't very hungry. But she took a few spoonfuls and held the familiar flavor in her mouth, thinking back to when she was a little girl and everything made more sense. When everything was less complicated.

The Chipies were chatting away about last summer's pool party, laughing about some trick they had pulled on Pilar's brothers. Livvie listened and smiled along with them. But out of the corner of her eye, she kept stealing glimpses of the mime. He was about fifteen feet away from her. She wondered if he had heard their conversation. In any case, Livvie was determined not to let what these girls had said about Lika keep her from celebrating his return.

When they had finished their glace and were getting ready to leave, Sylvie turned to Livvie and said quietly, "Why don't you walk back home with me a different way. I want to show you my favorite shop."

Mom was going to be late getting home again since she was having a drink after work with Jean-Pierre, so Livvie agreed. Plus, out of all these girls, she liked Sylvie by far the best.

As they all left the restaurant, the mime smiled and nodded at them. Livvie was the only one who smiled back.

Out on the sidewalk, Sylvie said to the rest of the group, "I want to take Olivia over to Z. You all go ahead."

They said their goodbyes and turned to leave. Livvie reached into her pocket and dropped some coins into the mime's bowl. She expected another nod, another smile. Instead the corners of his mouth turned down in an exaggerated sad face and he put his hands on his heart. He shuddered like he was crying. Livvie fought the urge to reach out her hand, to say something. Then Sylvie's arm slipped around hers and led her away, up one of the side streets off the Cours.

"Viens, Olivia," she said. "I wish Nicole wouldn't say things like that. She can be out of line sometimes. My maman says to ignore it. Her parents are going through a bad divorce and I think it's been hard on Nicole."

Livvie was still thinking of the mime's sad face. So she just nodded and Sylvie continued,

"My maman and Nicole's maman are best friends from way back when they were girls in Cassis, and I've known Nicole all my life. She's a little spoiled and can be a real pain sometimes, especially lately with how her dad has been treating her mom. So I wouldn't take anything she says too personally."

"My parents split up last summer, so I can sort of understand how she feels. But that's no excuse for saying those things about Malika. Nicole's probably never even had a conversation with her. Malika's such a nice girl."

"She seemed nice to me too. She was really shy when I sat near her though. She hardly said a word the whole year."

"Yeah, I guess she can be kind of shy at first. But when you get to know her, she's fun to talk to."

"Does she ever talk about her family?"

"Not really. Only that her parents make it kind of hard for her to be friends with anyone other than a Muslim."

"That is kind of strange, since she goes to a school where there are hardly any Muslims. Why wouldn't they want her to have friends?"

"Yeah, I don't know." Livvie's stomach started to hurt.

"Hey, here's that store I wanted to show you. It's the best. Nicole never wants to shop here though because she says we'd look too much like twins.

She can be such a pain. Kind of like a sister, I guess, since our moms are so close. She spends a lot of time at our house in Cassis ever since her grand-mère sold their house there."

"Do you like Cassis?"

"Are you kidding?—I love it. There's an incredible beach. And the glace is even better than at Le Bastide. It's less than an hour from Aix, so we spend practically the whole summer there. You'll have to come with me sometime."

"Thanks. That would be nice." They had reached where the road curved up toward Livvie's apartment. She slipped her arm out from Sylvie's and said, "Thanks again. I mean for explaining about Nicole."

"No problem. I'll see you tomorrow," Sylvie said in English.

They had been working on those expressions in English class lately, so Livvie laughed and said, "Very good! See you tomorrow."

As she walked the rest of the way home, Livvie thought about what Sylvie had said about Nicole and her family. It wasn't an excuse for how Nicole acted, but at least Livvie understood a little bit about where she was coming from.

One thing Sylvie said troubled Livvie, though, like a pebble in her shoe. As much as she tried to ignore it, it wouldn't go away. As she walked the final steps to her door, she almost felt like she was limping. It was what Sylvie had said about Lika's parents. How it was strange that they didn't want her to have friends at school. Lika herself had mentioned they didn't let her go to Sylvie's party. That made Livvie wonder if maybe they were—what was the word Mom used?—extremists. Maybe even terrorists. Terrorists. The word burned in Livvie's mind like a newspaper headline plastered everywhere you turn. She hoped with all her heart it wasn't true—it couldn't be true! The smiley face leered down at Livvie as she fumbled with her key. She quickly pushed open the door and ran up the stairs.

Chapter 24

The pebble was still there the next day. As soon as Livvie stepped out the front door to go to school, her feet didn't want to move. She forced herself to start walking, trying to still the questions racing through her mind. Could Lika's parents possibly be terrorists? Those people always in the news, bombing places or kidnapping people? What did that make Lika? Maybe she didn't even know about it. Or maybe she did and wished her parents were different. Or maybe none of it was true and everybody was imagining things.

Livvie was so lost in her thoughts on the way over to school that she was surprised when she was at the gate already. And just in time, because the gatekeeper was about to swing it shut. He raised his eyebrows at her as she slipped through. Livvie dreaded seeing Lika, but at the same time she was dying to know the truth about her family. Should she say anything to her about it? She didn't want to offend her. But maybe she wanted to talk about it. Maybe it was bothering her and she needed someone to talk to about it. Livvie had to find out.

She avoided the topic at lunch since there were too many people around, and tried to act completely normal. They sat near Thomas, who entertained the whole table with goofy jokes. Peahead was at their table too and competed with Thomas over who could get the biggest laugh. The server attempted to quiet them down whenever she stopped by their table, but that only egged them on even more.

By recess, Livvie couldn't wait any longer. "So, Lika," she said, trying to sound casual as they walked together toward their bench, "Did your parents ever ask you about the Eiffel Tower I gave you?"

Lika hesitated and quietly said, "I put it in my drawer. They don't know about it."

"But I thought you were going to—"

"I'm sorry," she said, looking at her feet. "I couldn't."

"Lika..." Livvie eased onto the bench and swallowed hard. Lika sat down and looked at Livvie, waiting for her to continue. Her big, dark eyes were sad, lonely pools. "Are your parents terrorists?" Livvie blurted out.

Lika gasped and jumped back against the bench, like she'd been slapped. Her eyes were even bigger now, but hard, like black onyx. "What are you saying?" she whispered.

"I, I didn't mean ... ."

But it was too late. Lika stood up from the bench and backed away, shaking her head. Her soft cheeks were bright red. She turned and ran across the courtyard toward the building and vanished behind the door.

Livvie sat there frozen, not knowing what to do. What had just happened? What had she done? Her heart flew around in her chest like a desperate bird. Like the starling that had gotten trapped in their laundry room last year. It had broken its wing from crashing into the ceiling and walls.

"Is everything okay, Olivia?"

Livvie looked up. Sylvie was standing in front of her. "Um, yeah. Malika didn't feel well." She couldn't believe she was lying to Sylvie now, on top of everything else.

"Do you want to come over with us? Pilar's showing us some photos. From her vacation in Spain."

"Um, sure." She felt light-headed as she stood up and followed Sylvie across the courtyard.

"Salut, Olivia!" Nicole called out, and the other girls echoed, "Salut! Salut!" The echo went on and on.

Livvie forced a smile and managed to say "Salut" back. Thankfully they turned back to the photos and burst into giggles about one of Pilar's brothers. Livvie stood beside Sylvie, apart from the group. She pretended to pay attention, but inside she was running to her apartment and throwing herself on her bed sobbing. What had she done? She wished she could take back those words! Then she would still be sitting on the bench with Lika, talking about something she cared about. Not standing around giggling over some boy she didn't even know. The girls' laughter rang in her ears. One of them thrust the photos in front of Livvie and she gazed down at the blurry, smiling faces, trying to focus. Struggling to keep the tears back and to slow down her pounding heart.

Finally the bell rang and she followed the Chipies back into the classroom. Lika was already there, sitting at her desk. She was writing something in a notebook and didn't look up at anyone. Livvie tried to catch her eye a few times, but Lika wouldn't look at her. Her head stayed down, focused on her work. When she did look up, her eyes were fixed on Monsieur Simon.

Livvie stared up at Monsieur too, but all she saw was Lika's face. Her onyx eyes full of hurt. She didn't hear anything he was saying either. In her head she replayed the conversation over and over. Wishing she could take it back. When the bell rang at the end of the day, Lika rushed out the door and disappeared. Livvie gathered up her things and let herself be carried out on the current of other students.

Chapter 25

That's how it went for the next few weeks. Lika refused to acknowledge Livvie. At recess, Lika brought a book with her and stood far away from their bench. She leaned against the wall at the edge of the courtyard near the gate and kept her face down, engrossed in the pages. At lunch she ate alone. Several times Livvie tried to talk to her, saying she was sorry, that she had made a mistake. But Lika completely ignored Livvie and kept on reading or eating her lunch.

Finally Livvie gave up and let herself be absorbed into Nicole's circle. It was easy to float along in their bubble, letting it take her where it went. Following their lead. Not saying much. Even though Nicole got on Livvie's nerves, there was something comforting about letting her take charge. Livvie sat with them at lunch and nodded at Nicole's stories, and stood in their circle at recess and laughed at her jokes. Sometimes she felt Sylvie looking at her in a puzzled way, but she brushed it off.

Nicole loved the attention and the new, submissive Livvie. "Olivia! I've saved a seat for you!" she called out at lunch, patting the chair beside her. "Olivia! We're going for pizza!" she cried, holding out her arm for Livvie while Pilar, Sylvie, and Gabrielle linked arms behind them.

Sometimes jealousy would flash across one of their faces, especially Gabrielle's. But because Livvie didn't care—about the jealousy, about being Nicole's chosen one, about any of it—it made her status as Nicole's favorite even more secure.

What she did care about was too hard to face. After Lika ignored her apologies, Livvie couldn't look at her any more. It hurt too much. But sometimes she couldn't help it and glanced over at Lika standing by herself, shoulders stooped, her face a plaster mask, and Livvie's heart ached. For Lika, for herself, for their friendship. At night in bed, she hugged her stuffed Clover to her chest and let the tears come, crying herself to sleep like she had when they first moved to Aix. Only this time, it hurt even more.

Livvie wished there was a way for her to fix it, but she didn't know how. There was no one she could talk to about it. Mom didn't even know Lika existed. She could try chatting online with Annabel about it, but Livvie didn't think she could possibly understand. Sylvie might, but Livvie didn't feel comfortable bringing it up with her. And Nicole would probably just dismiss the whole thing with the flick of her wrist, like she was brushing away a fly. So it was easier to go along with this new arrangement, pretending nothing was wrong. When, in fact, everything was.

Chapter 26

One day in late April Livvie opened the door to their apartment after school. It seemed quieter than usual as she slipped off her schoolbag, even though it was always empty when she got home. Right, Mom was getting home late again. Another date with Jean-Pierre. Mom's voice got all excited lately when she talked about him. She sounded like Nicole and Sylvie whenever Pilar's brothers were mentioned. She had started wearing a new perfume he liked, and stayed up late at night talking with him on her phone. Livvie would probably get to meet him soon, she said. A tiny part of Livvie was curious, but mostly she had no interest in meeting Mom's boyfriend.

Livvie didn't have much homework that day and for some reason didn't want to be in the apartment by herself. So she decided to walk over to Cours Mirabeau, maybe get some glace. She hadn't been down to the Cours in a while. Not since what happened with Lika. She hadn't wanted to see the mime because it would have made her feel worse.

But on this particular day, she hoped he would be there, his enchanting silver hands speaking comfort. Please let me see him, she repeated to herself as she walked through town to the Cours. When she turned toward the café, her heart sank. He wasn't there. But his white box was, looking like a mysterious package gleaming all by itself on the sidewalk. He had to be around somewhere. Livvie scanned the crowd on the street and in the outdoor café. There he was. Sitting at a table by himself drinking a Perrier. She stood looking at him until he glanced at her and gazed back. Before she thought about what she was doing, she walked directly over to him.

"Bonjour, Monsieur."

"Bonjour, Mademoiselle." His voice was warm and friendly, like his eyes.

"May I sit down?" Livvie pointed to the chair beside him.

"Of course," he said, sounding not at all surprised. "You have an accent. Where are you from?"

Not this again. Why did it matter where she was from? Why did everyone have to be from somewhere? "The United States," she said quietly.

"Ah, you're American. That's what I thought. America is a magnificent country."

"Have you been there?"

"Why, yes. Several times. My son lives there. He's married to an American. I was there this past winter for a few months."

So that's where he was. Livvie would have never guessed.

"You know what I admire about America? The spirit of your people. Their openness, their imagination, their bravery, their heart. I hope America never loses those qualities. It's what made her great and, without that, well, the world will be a different place."

Livvie didn't know what to say, so she mumbled, "Merci." A waiter stopped by the table and she ordered some glace.

The mime took a sip of his Perrier. His mouth left a faint silver mark on the rim of his glass. "You've been in town for a while," he said. "What brings you to France?"

"I came here with my mom after my parents split up. She's always wanted to live in France, ever since she studied here in college. So here we are."

"Your mother picked a lovely city. I've lived here all my life and it never stops charming me."

"Have you always been a mime?"

"Oh, no. I taught high school history for thirty years. When I retired, I was driving my wife crazy with nothing to do. And I missed being around people. So I decided to become a mime. I never imagined how much I would love it. The money is merely a bonus. My wife and I use it to travel every winter. Even without the money, I'd still do it."

"It seems fun," Livvie said, instantly regretting it. What a dumb thing to say. Out of all the things she wanted to say to him. To ask him. The waiter set her dish of ice cream down in front of her and she tried to think of a better reply.

"Yes, it is fun." He paused, looking out at the people walking by his box. "But it's more than fun. It's a way of communicating that overcomes barriers. People from all over the world respond to me in the same way, you see, because miming is a universal language. Laughter, joy, sorrow, love, fear, surprise, wonder. The whole human experience. There's no such thing as miming in French, or English, or Chinese, or Arabic. I wish our world leaders would learn this simple lesson. I think there would be a lot more peace in the world if they did. You know what I mean, oui?"

What he said made more sense than anything Livvie had heard in months. "Miming is a universal language," she repeated, nodding.

"Even though we all might be different in other ways," he continued. "Like religion. Or skin color. Or nationality. But different is okay. It's more than okay. Different is good. The world would be a lot less interesting if everyone were exactly the same, oui?"

Livvie kept nodding. Her ice cream started to melt in its dish.

"But what's more important than our differences is what we share, as human beings." The mime paused and took another sip. "You know, I couldn't help but overhear some of your conversation a few weeks ago. You were sitting here in this café. Tell me, did you ever resolve your problem?"

"What do you mean?" Livvie looked up at his face. At its bumps and creases softened by silver paint.

"I remember you were upset about a friend of yours. A Muslim girl."

As soon as he said that, something in Livvie gave way. Like how, on a wintry day in Vermont after a big snow storm, snow would be everywhere and their metal roof would be piled high with it. Then the sun would come out and warm things up and, all of a sudden, the snow would begin to slide off the roof. They would hear it from inside. Huge thundering booms of white that exploded into a million particles outside their windows. One after another. Until the roof was clear and green and shining amid all that whiteness.

It was like that. She told him everything. One sliding, thundering, exploding boom after another. She told him about coming to France and how alone she felt. About how she met Malika on their bench. She told him about the books, and their miming, and the Chipies. She told him how they both love his Thinker pose. And how she saw the real sculpture in Paris. She told him about Dad's visit and the miniature Eiffel Tower, and about what Mom said about extremists, and what Nicole and Pilar and Sylvie said at the café. Finally, she told him what she said to Lika, and how now Lika wouldn't even look at her. And how it broke her heart and she wished she could take it back. But she couldn't.

Throughout it all, the mime sat listening. Sometimes smoothing his silver hair with a silver hand. Sometimes nodding his head. When Livvie finally finished, and relief, shining and green, spread throughout her body, he said, "Well, Mademoiselle, it sounds to me like you know what you must do."

"Yes, but how?"

"I think you'll find a way. You're brave, imaginative, and most importantly you have a good heart," he said with a smile. "And now, I have to get back to work. My fans are waiting. I can at least indulge them another half an hour before I need to get home."

"But, but, Monsieur…"

"Be like The Thinker. You can do it. But, please, let me buy your glace."

"Merci, Monsieur. And for the glace too."

"You're welcome. You may call me Albert."

"Okay, Albert. I'm Olivia. Livvie for short."

"Pleased to meet you, Livvie. Let me know how it goes."

"I will."

He walked back over to his box and sat down. Looking over at Livvie, he gave her a wink and got into his Thinker pose. A small group gathered around him. Japanese tourists snapping photos, a cluster of nuns in their habits, a family with small children.

Livvie hadn't realized how late it had gotten—it was already 6:30—so she hurried home hoping Mom wouldn't be worried. She didn't want to have to explain where she'd been. Mom wouldn't be thrilled to hear she'd been sitting in a café with the mime. Although maybe if she told Mom about him, she wouldn't be upset. After all, he was a retired teacher. Had a wife and son. Liked to travel like she did. He was so far from what people had imagined about him. Mom and her comments about low-life street performers, and the Chipies thinking he was some kind of a thief! And here he was just a regular guy, a nice, old man. Older than Livvie had thought, but it was hard to tell his age, or anything else about him, under all that silver paint. He even kind of reminded her of Grandpa.

Relief was still spreading through Livvie, warming her all over, as she practically skipped down the sidewalk. She had no idea how she was going to fix things with Lika, but at least she was beginning to feel like there was a way. The mime—or Albert—thought so. All she had to do was figure out how. One thing she did know was that Lika missed their friendship too. Underneath her hardened mask, Livvie knew she was sad too.

Chapter 27

When Livvie got back to the apartment, it was still empty. That was strange. Mom should have been home by now. Whenever she went out after work with Jean-Pierre, she was always home by 6:45. It was getting close to dinnertime, Livvie had school the next day, and where was Mom? This was so typical of her. Just when Livvie needed Mom, when she was ready to talk with her about something important, Mom wasn't there. Or she was on her cell phone. Or thinking about the next time she was going to see Jean-Pierre. Here Livvie was excited to talk with her about Albert, and maybe ready to tell her all about Lika. Maybe even ask for her advice. And she wasn't there.

Livvie tried to reach Mom on her phone, but for some reason she didn't answer it. That was very odd. She mustn't have wanted anyone disturbing her romantic date with Jean-Pierre, even her own daughter. What if Livvie had been kidnapped or something? Livvie left a short message for her to call home.

Although she was hungry now, Livvie didn't want to eat dinner by herself and decided she'd give Mom a half an hour. If she still wasn't home, Livvie would call someone else and go over to their house. Nicole was only a few blocks away and would probably love the company. Sylvie wasn't far away either.

To pass the time, Livvie went into her bedroom to do some homework. As she grabbed her dictionary off the bookshelf, her eyes stopped at the book leaning beside it. Its blue spine glowed like a beacon. Livvie reached down, slowly slid it off the shelf, and opened up the front cover. There it was. Malika's name in pencil on the inside cover, and below it her phone number. In darker pencil. Asking Livvie to call her.

A half an hour hadn't passed yet, but now that Livvie had gotten the idea in her head to call Lika, she had to do it. As she quickly dialed the number and listened to the phone ringing, her heart drummed. She held her breath.

"Allô?" said a woman's voice on the other end.

"May I please speak to Malika?" Livvie said exhaling, using her best French r's.

There was a long pause and the woman said, "One moment, please."

Some muffled talking hummed in the background, then Lika's voice spoke into the phone, hesitant and questioning. "Allô?"

"Hi, Lika. It's Livvie." Please don't hang up, please don't hang up, Livvie kept herself from saying.

The phone was silent. Livvie's blood thumped in her ears. The line crackled and she strained to hear if Lika was still there. Finally Lika said, "Oui?"

With that one word, Livvie knew she had a chance. So without a plan or a strategy, she started talking. "I'm so glad you didn't hang up. I'm so, so glad. I know you must be wondering why I'm calling and it's … it's because I miss you. I didn't realize how much until I was talking with the mime today. His name is Albert and he's really nice. I wish you could have been with me." Livvie paused. The line was silent again. "Lika? Are you there?"

"Oui."

"I'm so glad. That you're there. I'm here by myself and I'm not sure where my mom is. I mean, she's out with Jean-Pierre. Remember I told you about him? Anyway, she's not here and I just got back from talking with the mime, and I … I wanted to talk to you."

"You met the mime?"

"Yeah, Albert. It was amazing. I can't wait to tell you about it. Can I come over?" The words were out of Livvie's mouth before she realized what she was asking. She didn't even know where Lika lived. And what were her parents going to think of some American girl barging in on them?

"Hold on. Let me ask my parents."

Livvie couldn't believe it. She was asking them! There was more muffled talking in the background, animated this time. Livvie waited for Lika to get back on the phone and say, "Sorry, not tonight. Not ever." She held her breath again and when Lika said, "Okay. You can come," Livvie let out a huge gasp.

"Thank you, Lika!"

"We're on Boulevard Jean Jaurès. Across from Thermes Sextius in an apartment building. It's number 225. We're on the third floor, apartment 3B."

"Okay. I'll be right over."

Livvie grabbed her jacket and ran out the door. When she got to the bottom of the stairs, she remembered she hadn't left a note for Mom. But Mom hadn't left one for her either. Plus she didn't want to waste any time getting over to Lika's house and she could always call her from there.

She flew up Cours Saint Louis and past the turn-off to school. It was nearing dusk and most cars had their headlights turned on. She dodged in and out of people walking home with baguettes tucked under their arms and made her way toward Thermes Sextius, the old Roman baths. They were a big tourist site in Aix and easy to find. She and Mom had explored the ruins there when they first moved to town and were checking out the neighborhood. A jogger sped by Livvie so she picked up her pace.

Finally Livvie saw the ruins coming up on the left, glowing eerily in the dusk. The crumbling, white monuments to a previous civilization rose up from the ground like ghosts. A few straggling tourists were still wandering around in them. Right across the street was a four-story, new building with big balconies on every floor. It was number 225. Lights shined from the windows, and the walkway was lined with beds of pansies. Livvie followed a woman pushing a stroller through the double glass doors into a bright lobby. An elevator dinged open and she stepped in beside the stroller.

With a trembling finger, Livvie pressed the button for the third floor. The baby squealed and laughed as the elevator rose. Livvie's heart pounded and she started to think this was a bad idea. What if her parents were expecting a French girl? What would they say when they found out she was American? What if Lika told them what Livvie had said?

The door dinged again and slid open. Livvie followed the woman and baby out of the elevator, and the baby waved as they turned down the hallway. The door in front of Livvie was marked 3A, so 3B had to be the one beside it. Livvie stood in the middle of the hallway staring at the entrance to Lika's apartment.

The woman with the baby fiddled with her keys a few doors down. She looked up at Livvie and asked, "Can I help you? Are you looking for someone?"

"Um, non. Merci. It's right here."

"Bien," she said and smiled. She and the baby disappeared behind a door.

Bien, Livvie told herself, good. This is good. She willed her feet to step up to 3B. Her hand to knock.

The door opened quickly and Lika stood before her. This was the first time they had looked each other in the eyes in weeks and Livvie was relieved not to see onyx. But she wasn't sure what was there in its place.

"Salut, Lika."

"Salut, Livvie."

"Thanks for having me over."

Lika paused, her hand on the doorknob. "Come in."

Livvie stepped into a foyer. The floor was covered by a colorful, woven rug. It was similar to rugs she had seen being sold at the market by a jovial North African vendor. A painting of a city by the water hung on one of the walls. Glistening white buildings sloped up from a turquoise bay.

"You can leave your shoes here," Lika said, pointing under a small table. Her brown school shoes rested there along with a few others. She was wearing some intricately beaded slippers that made Livvie's old socks look graceless and plain.

Lika led Livvie into the next room, a large living room smelling faintly of cinnamon and cloves. A dark-haired man sat on a couch reading a newspaper. He looked up as they came in, closed the paper, and stood.

"Papa, this is my friend Olivia."

"Bonsoir, Olivia," he said, holding out his hand.

"Bonsoir, Monsieur," Livvie said, shaking his hand and smiling politely. His eyes were large and dark like Lika's, but not onyx. Livvie wasn't sure what she saw in them either.

"So, you go to school with Malika?"

"Oui, Monsieur." He wore a navy blue blazer and had a dignified look.

"And you're not French. I hear an accent. Where are you from?"

Here it comes. Au revoir. Good-bye. "The United States."

"Ah." Something flickered through his eyes. But he merely said, "I have some students from the United States. I teach at the university."

Livvie smiled, a real smile, and nodded. Lika's mother came into the room wiping her hands on a dishtowel. Livvie had never seen her without a headscarf on, and her black hair was long and wavy like Lika's. "Bonsoir," she said, extending her hand. "I'm Madame Nasri."

"Bonsoir, Madame. I'm Olivia."

"I understand you're staying for dinner?"

"Oui, merci."

"I wish I'd known earlier. I would have prepared something more. We're just having a lamb stew."

"I'm sorry. I mean, that's okay. It sounds delicious."

"We'll eat in about forty-five minutes. Malika, did you get your homework finished?"

"Oui, Maman. We'll be in my room."

Livvie followed Lika down a hallway lined with photographs, suppressing the urge to giggle. That had all seemed so normal. Even more normal than her family. It could have been at Annabel's house, except for the shoes. Annabel's little brother Connor was always running through the house in his dirty sneakers driving their mom nuts.

Lika's bedroom was not what Livvie was expecting either. It was painted light blue and had pretty white furniture. The bed was covered in a blue and white floral bedspread, one of those fresh-looking, quilted French bedspreads Mom had been wanting to get for her bed. Some interesting framed tiles hung on one wall, decorated with blue and white geometric patterns of swirling vines and flowers. A colorful woven rug lay on the floor, like the one in the foyer. And the curtains were made out of an exotic-looking gauzy fabric. Lika's desk and bookshelf were all very neat and orderly, which wasn't surprising. There were no precarious piles of books and, unlike Livvie's own room, nothing strewn around on the floor. Livvie could understand how Lika's parents would notice if the Eiffel Tower suddenly appeared. But they hadn't seemed as if they would mind.

"What is it?" Lika sat on her bed watching Livvie take in her room.

"I like your room. It's pretty."

"Merci." She shrugged her shoulders.

Livvie walked over to Lika's bookshelf and slid out the book she had given her. "That's where I got your number. In the book you gave me."

Lika nodded. "So, you said you talked to the mime today?"

"Yes, can you believe it? His name is Albert and he's so nice. He was sitting at the café and I went right up to him and sat down and we talked for over an hour!"

"No way. What did you talk about?"

"All kinds of things. He used to be a teacher. He's retired and does the miming for fun."

"A teacher?"

"Yeah. And he's married and has a son who lives in the United States. That's where he was this winter. I couldn't believe it. He was so different from what I had imagined."

Livvie's words hung in the air as Lika looked down at her slippers and slowly moved her feet in small circles on the floor.

He was so different from what I had imagined. Like Lika's family. Livvie walked over and sat down beside her on the bed.

"Lika, I'm so sorry about what I said. I didn't mean it. I guess I was confused about a lot of things, and when you were worried about your parents finding out the Eiffel Tower was from me, I guess I thought … I don't know. It was wrong and I'm really sorry. Will you ever forgive me?"

When Lika looked up, her eyes were deep, watery pools of sorrow. She didn't say anything. Livvie's own eyes welled up with tears. "I can understand if you can't. I'm so sorry, Lika."

Livvie reached over and put her arms around Lika, sobbing. Lika's shoulders softened and shook, and she put her arms around Livvie too. They cried together for several minutes, holding each other. Finally Lika whispered, "I forgive you, Livvie."

Chapter 28

Livvie and Lika sat holding each other for a long time. Until their shoulders stopped shaking and their breathing slowed down. Only then did they loosen their arms.

"I told Albert about how you and I mimed at first, when I didn't know any French," Livvie said. "That's what he likes best about miming. How it's a universal language. How everybody feels the same basic things deep down. It doesn't matter where they're from. Or what their religion is."

Lika nodded.

"You're parents seem nice, Lika."

"They're okay. Maman can be a little too protective sometimes."

"At least she cares. My mom's too wrapped up in her own life to worry about me. She doesn't even know I'm over here. Now that she has Jean-Pierre, that's all she cares about."

"Really? That must be hard. I don't know why I was so worried about the Eiffel Tower. It probably wouldn't have been a big deal. They just get upset sometimes about everything going on in the world. I didn't know how they'd react to me being friends with an American. As if you're all alike. But they didn't mind when I asked them if you could come over. Maman actually seemed happy about it. She said I'd been too quiet the past few weeks. But she wished she'd known in advance so she could make a nicer dinner." Lika leaned back on her elbows and smiled.

"You look a lot like her when she doesn't have her headscarf on."

"Yeah, people used to say that all the time. She's been wearing it for the past few years. Ever since Grand-père died."

"You mean, like in honor of him?" Livvie leaned back on her elbows too.

"Sort of. He and my other grandparents came over to France from Algeria. They lived in Algiers, the city in the painting. In the foyer."

"Oh, yeah. It looked like a nice city."

"It is, but they were poor and wanted a better life. So they came here. Maman and Papa were both born in France. They've worked hard and have been lucky, so they've done well. Although in France, you know...."

"What?"

"People don't always treat Muslims the same as other French people. Even though we're French citizens just like they are. And about one-tenth of the population is Muslim. Everyone is supposed to be treated equally here, but that's not always true." Lika lay down on the bed and crossed her hands behind her head. She looked up at the ceiling and continued. "So when Grand-père died, and with the struggles Muslims are facing in France and in the world, Maman decided to start wearing the headscarf. To feel more connected to our heritage. To Islam."

Livvie lay back with her hands behind her head too and thought about her own relatives. How her great-grandparents had come over on a boat across the Atlantic. From Ireland, Germany, and Austria. In search of the American Dream. How they were all poor, but worked hard and carved out a better life. And how, sure, Livvie's family ate sauerkraut and sausages sometimes on holidays, and she always remembered to wear green on Saint Patrick's Day. But her ancestors' home countries weren't an important part of her family's identity. They were American more than anything else. Livvie wondered, though, if some Americans felt like Lika did. Like they weren't treated the same way. Almost as if they weren't American. It made sense that Lika's family would want to keep their Muslim identity alive.

"It must be hard to feel like an outsider even in your own country," Livvie said. "I mean, my relatives all came over to America from other countries too. Like most people in America. We've never felt like outsiders though. But I guess some people might. Depending on their race. Or their religion."

"Mhmm. What about your religion? Is it important to you and your family?"

"I'm Christian. I mean, that's my family's tradition. But we only go to church for holidays, so I don't feel a strong connection to it. I wish I did in a way. Some of my relatives and friends back in the US are really involved in their churches. I feel a little left out sometimes, like there's this whole world associated with it that I don't understand." The cinnamon aroma Livvie smelled earlier was getting stronger and deeper. Her stomach growled. "How about your family?"

"We go to the mosque every week. It's very important to my family. We get together with all my cousins and other relatives there. But my parents don't strictly follow all the rules of Islam."

"Do you think you'll wear a headscarf like your mom?"

"The hijab? I don't know. I still have a few years to decide. Maman and Papa say it's my choice. I'm not sure what I'll do."

They lay on the bed and continued to look up at the ceiling, both lost in their own thoughts. There was a knock on the door and Lika's mom called, "Malika? Time to wash up for dinner."

They slowly got up but, before going out into the hall, Lika walked over to her desk. She opened the drawer and took out the Eiffel Tower. She placed it on top of her desk, saying, "Voilà. That's better." And then in English, "It's good."

Chapter 29

As they entered the dining room, a warm, spicy deliciousness filled the air. Lika's dad was placing a large soup tureen onto the table, which was set with a pale orange tablecloth and matching napkins. Ceramic dishes decorated with swirling green, blue, yellow, and orange were laid out for the four of them. The dishes' vivid geometric pattern was similar to the tiles in Lika's bedroom.

Lika's mom put a basket filled with sliced baguette on the table and said, pointing, "Olivia, you may sit there, as the guest of honor."

Lika took the seat across from Livvie, and her mom and dad sat at opposite ends of the table.

"How long have you been living in France?" Lika's dad asked, serving Livvie a ladleful of the lamb stew.

"Since August."

"You came with your family?"

"With my mom. My parents are divorced, so my dad's back in the US."

"Is your mother with the university?" Lika's mom asked, passing the bread.

"No, she's works for Dell. The computer company." Livvie tasted a spoonful of the stew. Mint and cinnamon danced around in her mouth.

"Vraiment," Lika's mom said smiling. "I'm an engineer and our firm does some work with them. What is her name?"

"Diane Renner."

"Diane Renner. I'll have to remember that next time I have a project with Dell."

"Olivia is from Vermont. Up on the border with Canada," Lika said.

"Vermont. It's very cold there, isn't it?" her dad said.

"Yes, it gets really cold in the winter. But the summer and fall are beautiful."

That's how it went for the rest of the dinner. They chatted about Vermont, and what Livvie liked about Aix, and school. They had a nice, friendly, comfortable conversation. Lika's dad refilled Livvie's bowl when it was empty and, at the end of the meal, Lika's mom placed a platter of fancy cookies in front of her saying, "Guests get to choose first."

Livvie took one that looked like a delicate bird's nest with chopped nuts inside. When she bit into it, honey oozed onto her tongue.

After dessert Lika's mom said, "You should probably be getting home soon, Olivia. You're maman will worry."

Suddenly Livvie remembered she had never called home. Mom was not going to be happy about that. But Livvie didn't want to get into it with her on the phone at Lika's house, so she decided to deal with it when she got back to the apartment.

"I'll walk you back," Lika's dad said. "Malika, why don't you come along."

At the door, when Livvie thanked Lika's mom, she leaned over to kiss Livvie on both cheeks, saying, "We were happy to have you. Please come again."

"Merci beaucoup, Madame. I'd like that."

They stepped into the elevator and, as the door slid shut, Livvie marveled at how much had changed since she had ridden the elevator up. How she and Lika were friends again. Closer than ever. How Livvie knew her parents now and how nice they were. Maybe she and Mom could even have them all over to their apartment for dinner sometime.

They walked through the lobby and into the balmy spring night. It was dark out and the street was quiet. On the other side, though, near the Roman ruins, some people were shining flashlights. The beams of light swept through the decaying stone structures making them even more desolate than usual. Men's voices called out urgently, and one woman's. The woman's voice sounded strangely like Mom's. But it couldn't be her. What would she be doing out there?

"Did you find anything?" the woman cried, her voice breaking. It was definitely Mom.

"Mom?" Livvie called out. "Mom, is that you?"

"Livvie! She's over there!" Mom cried.

The flashlights zeroed in on Livvie, Lika, and Monsieur Nasri. Feet thundered on the pavement. "Arrêtez! Stop!" a man's voice shouted.

All at once, the group was upon them. Mom hugged Livvie fiercely and screamed at Lika's dad, "What did you do to her?"

The men, two policemen, grabbed hold of him and bombarded him with questions. "Who are you? Where are your papers? What are you doing with these girls?"

Lika yelped like she'd been struck. Livvie pushed Mom away and shouted, "Wait! He didn't do anything! He's Malika's dad! My friend's dad!"

The policemen had Lika's father by both arms and were shining the flashlights in his face. It looked oddly familiar to Livvie, that face, those eyes. Suddenly she recognized it. It was the same as Lika's when Livvie asked if her parents were terrorists. The policemen's own faces glowed like fallen moons.

"Let him go," Livvie pleaded. "He didn't do anything wrong."

Lika was sobbing and one policeman asked her, "Mademoiselle, is this true? Is he your father?"

"Yes," she cried. "He's my Papa! And he did nothing wrong!"

The policemen released his arms. He brushed them off and straightened his jacket, as if he was wiping off dirt. In the dim light of the streetlamp, his face struggled to regain composure, his eyes still hard as onyx. But burning, like onyx on fire. Lika lunged toward him and he grasped her tightly.

"Livvie, what's going on? Where were you?" Mom's voice, now angry, pulled Livvie's attention away from Lika and her dad.

"Where was I? Where were you, Mom? You never came home, so I went over to my friend's house for dinner!"

"Your friend's house?" Mom stared at Lika.

"Yes, my friend's house. This is my friend Malika."

The policemen shook their heads and one of them muttered, "Crazy Americans."

"I'm sorry," Mom said to them. "It looks like it was all a big misunderstanding. Thank you for your help."

They turned off their flashlights and disappeared into the darkness, grumbling.

Lika and her dad were still clutching each other, and Livvie wanted to throw her arms around both of them too. But not around Mom. What right did Mom have to be angry? Plus now she had made Lika's dad feel like a criminal.

"This is Malika's dad, Mom, Monsieur Nasri."

"I'm sorry about the misunderstanding, Monsieur," Mom said.

Lika's father nodded but didn't say anything.

Mom continued, glaring at Livvie, "A neighbor, Madame Durand, saw Olivia sitting in a café with that mime from Cours Mirabeau. And when you didn't come home, Olivia, I got so worried that maybe he'd done something. I ran down there and he was gone, so I called the police. They checked his house and you weren't there, so we've been looking all over. Then they got a call about some people seen up here by the ruins after hours. What were you doing with that mime anyway?"

"Mom, I'll explain about all that later. Malika and her family have been so nice to me. I've had such a great time at their house, and I don't want this to ruin it." Livvie looked at Lika pleading for forgiveness, again.

But Lika looked up at her dad, who said in a stiff voice, "It's late. We should get inside."

They turned toward the building, their arms still wrapped around each other.

Chapter 30

"Bonsoir, Lika!" Livvie called after them, but there was no response. The street was unbearably quiet. Mom put her arm around Livvie and tried to guide her toward home. But she wriggled out of Mom's grasp.

"Livvie? What is it? Can you blame me for being worried when I had no idea where you were?"

"I had no idea where you were either, Mom. Didn't you get my message?"

"What message?"

"On your cell phone."

"Oh, Liv, my battery died this afternoon and with everything that's gone on I haven't gotten a chance to recharge it. But that's no excuse for you to go running around all over town. Hanging out with street performers and going over to strangers' apartments!"

A pair of motorcycles screamed past them on the street. Livvie stomped along the sidewalk in silence. Mom walked beside her, trying to keep up, her arms crossed over her chest. Her pointy-toed shoes clip-clopped on the pavement. "Livvie, I was worried," she said.

Livvie kept stomping in silence. The rumble of the motorcycles could still be heard in the distance.

Finally, as they passed the turn-off toward school, Mom said, "Look. I'm sorry I was late. But next time, please leave a note."

"None of this would have happened if you hadn't been out with Jean-Pierre again."

"Is that what this is all about? You're upset about Jean-Pierre?"

"It's not Jean-Pierre, Mom. It's everything. You never listen to me. I mean, even when you're listening. You don't hear what I'm trying to say!"

The night air was no longer balmy and Livvie shivered.

"I do listen. I just wish you'd share more things with me. Like this friend Malika. You've never mentioned her before. You can't expect me to know what's going on in your life if you don't tell me about it."

Livvie couldn't hold it all in any longer. She burst out crying, right there on the street, screaming at Mom, "I try to tell you, but you're only interested in what you want to hear! You wanted me to be friends with Nicole and her group! Those perfect French girls. So that's what I did. But you know what, Mom? They aren't always very nice people. Malika is so much nicer, and more interesting, and a better friend, but you're like everybody else! Just because she's different, because she's a Muslim, you don't think she's worthy of my friendship. Isn't that true, Mom? Isn't it?"

Livvie had stopped walking, so Mom stopped too. They stood facing each other in front of the darkened hair salon on their block. The photos of models wearing the latest hair styles peered out at them from the window as if disturbed from their sleep. But Livvie didn't care if she woke up the whole street.

"You want to know about the mime? I'll tell you about the mime. He's my other friend here. His name is Albert. And you are so wrong about him! You think he's some sort of perverted low-life. Not worth your time. You don't know anything! I can't believe you brought the police over to his house tonight. Now he'll probably never talk to me again either." Livvie took a deep, jagged breath, her sobs making the air catch in her throat.

Mom was staring at her, but she continued, "I came over here with you so you could live out your dream of a glamorous French life. And it hasn't been easy for me, Mom. Not knowing anybody. Not speaking the language. Not having Dad. Or Clover. Or any of my friends. But I've tried my best to make it work. I've tried to be a 'good daughter.' But now it's all ruined with the two people I care about the most here!"

In the light of the streetlamp, Mom's face softened and scrunched up. Tears spilled over onto her cheeks. Livvie's mind flashed back to the last time she saw Mom cry. It was a few years ago when Grandpa died. Even after Dad left last summer, Livvie couldn't remember seeing Mom cry.

"I'm sorry, Livvie. I never should have made you do this. It was selfish of me. I didn't realize how hard this whole move has been on you." Mom reached over to hug Livvie, and this time Livvie let her. "If you want us to move back to Vermont, that's okay. We can do that. It's unfair of me to force you to live here."

"But that's not what I'm saying. I don't want to move back. At least not now. I mean, maybe in a few years. But I'm not ready to go back yet." As soon as the words were out of her mouth, they surprised both Livvie and Mom.

"Okay… if that's what you want, Livvie. Is it really what you want?" Mom pulled back and looked directly into Livvie's eyes.

"Yes. I don't want to move back," Livvie repeated, sure of the words this time.

"Okay. But we need to make some changes. I need to make some changes. I know that now. You're shivering. Let's get home, sweetie." Mom kept one arm around Livvie as they walked the rest of the way to their apartment.

"I'm sorry I didn't leave a note, Mom."

"And I'm sorry I was late. I didn't get home until around seven. I should have called."

"We must have just missed each other. That's about when I left for Malika's."

"I went downstairs to the Durands' to see if you were there, and that's when Madame Durand told me she saw you with the mime. Or 'that street person who mimes,' as she put it. She got me so worried."

"Poor Albert. I hope the police weren't mean to him." Livvie pictured his sad face, his hands on his heart.

"They weren't. But now I feel badly about it. He seemed like a sweet man. He was worried that you were missing."

"I'll have to go explain everything to him. Maybe you could come. Meet him, I mean."

"Sure, Liv. If he's a friend of yours, I'd like to do that. I'd like to get to know Malika too.

They reached their door and turned up the stairs, too tired to take off their shoes. As they passed by the landing in front of the Durands' door, it opened a crack and Madame Durand peeked her head out. "I see you found your daughter. Is everything okay? "

"Oui, Madame. Merci. Everything's fine. She was with a friend. It was all a big misunderstanding."

Her forehead wrinkled up. She shook her head and let out a big sigh, no doubt thinking "crazy Americans" like the policemen. She reached out her hand and squeezed Livvie's arm, saying, "Poor child." Then she glanced down at their shoes. Fortunately they were clean, so she nodded her approval and closed the door. Livvie and Mom looked at each other and giggled. They covered their mouths with their hands to keep from giggling too loudly as they walked the rest of the way upstairs to their door.

As they stepped inside their apartment, fatigue hit Livvie like a speeding TGV. All of the worry and anticipation and frustration and release of the day's events hit her full on.

Mom must have read her thoughts because she said, "How about if we both take tomorrow off, Livvie? It's a Friday, and I think a long weekend together would do us both some good."

"Yeah, good idea."

Before Livvie went into her bedroom, Mom gave her a big hug and said, "I love you, Liv. I love you so much."

"I love you too, Mom."

Chapter 31

The next morning Livvie woke up late to the sun streaming through her window. At first she was disoriented, but soon the previous night's events came flooding back. It was Friday, she remembered, and she and Mom were staying home. She took a deep breath and rolled over, relieved to not have to go to school. Because she would have to face Lika. And after what had happened the night before, Lika might refuse to speak to her again.

The sun's warm fingers were insistent on her back so Livvie sat up in bed and bunched up her pillow behind her. She looked out her window into the light bouncing off the craggy peak of Sainte Victoire in the distance. The mountain sparkled and shimmered like silver. What would it be like to hike that mountain? To climb all the way to the top, like she used to do with Dad on Camel's Hump in Vermont. Was it all silver and sparkly when you're up on the summit?

She heard shuffling in the foyer and Mom appeared in the doorway wearing her bathrobe. "Good morning, Livvie. How'd you sleep?"

"Good. I was wiped out."

"Me too. But I stayed up for a while thinking about everything. There's a lot to think about. How about if I make us a big, hearty breakfast? Omelets and sausage?"

"Yeah, that sounds great."

Livvie stayed in bed a little longer, letting the sun warm her all over. Mom was right. There was a lot to think about. Like how all this time Livvie thought she was wanting to be back in Vermont. But how last night she had said she wanted to stay in Aix. It was true, she realized. She did want to stay. Maybe not for forever, but at least for a while. This was her home now. Even if things were wrecked with Lika and Albert.

Mom called in, "Let's eat out on the balcony. It's such a beautiful day."

Livvie got up and helped Mom carry the breakfast outside. Sainte Vic-toire looked even more dazzling from out there, a massive silver stone rising up like enchanted Oz out of the spring-green countryside surrounding it. Liv-vie was awed by how it changed color, depending on the time of day, the light.

"I've been thinking a lot about what you said last night." Mom sat down in the chair beside Livvie. "Are you sure you want to stay in France? Because if you want us to go back, I'm fine with that."

"Yeah, Mom, I really do want to stay."

"I was thinking we could at least take a trip back to the US this summer. For a few weeks. You could visit Dad in Boston and we could spend some time in Vermont. Would you like that?"

"Yeah, that would be good. For a few weeks." Livvie heard some kids laughing and shouting, and wondered if the sounds were coming from school. It would be about the time that the younger grades had recess.

"You know, I admire how open you've been to meeting all kinds of peo-ple here," Mom said. "So much more than I've been. Sure, I've met people, but the same kinds of people I've always known. I wish I were more like you in that way, Liv. You've gotten to know the French culture much better than I have in my safe, little world at work."

"What about Jean-Pierre? He's French."

"He may be French, but other than that he's not very different from any other man I've been involved with. As I said last night, I need to make some changes. I know I need to be here for you more. And for myself too. The last thing I need to do is lose myself in another man." Mom paused and pushed a piece of sausage around on her plate. "That's what happened with Dad. I gave up so many of my own interests and became too dependent on him and his world that I lost myself. No wonder he left me for someone else."

Livvie almost choked on a piece of her omelet. "What? What do you mean?"

"I didn't want to tell you before. I thought Dad should be the one to do that. But you deserve to know. I don't want to keep things from you anymore. You're no longer a little kid." Mom took a deep breath and quietly said, "Dad left me for Becky Catrell. That new DJ."

"Dad left you for someone else?"

"Yes, but, Livvie, what I'm saying is that I was partially responsible. I realize that now. I gave up too much of myself for him, and I didn't understand how resentful I was about it. How angry I was at him. At myself. How I was driving him away. And then he fell in love with someone else." Mom's breath shuddered, like she was trying not to cry. "Maybe I shouldn't be telling you all this. It's complicated and I don't expect you to understand."

Livvie gazed out at Sainte Victoire, trying to comprehend Mom's words, to get her mind around them. How had all this been going on and Livvie had no idea? The mountain looked so solid and permanent. Like it had been there forever and always would be. Even though it might appear to change color, the mountain itself stayed the same. Regardless of daily or weekly events, or even the series of civilizations that had risen and fallen in its shadow. All those different groups of people Livvie had learned about at school who had called this land their home as the country evolved. At least Sainte Victoire seemed permanent. Not shifting and sifting and changing, like the ground beneath Livvie's feet did everywhere she turned these days.

"I thought you both decided to split up. That you wanted to come over here," Livvie finally said.

"No. I decided to come over here after he followed Becky to Boston. I wanted a fresh start. I should have been upfront with you. But I think maybe I wasn't being upfront with myself. I don't want to make the same mistake again."

"You mean with Jean-Pierre? Are you breaking up with him?

"I don't know. I need to work all that out. But I do know he's not my top priority. You are. And I also need to take better care of myself."

"Like the smoking?"

"How did you know about that?" Mom's fork stopped in mid-air.

"Mom, I'm not stupid. I could smell it on your clothes."

"Well, I'm going to stop. Today. No more sneaking out on the balcony at night to cry and smoke a cigarette. No more feeling sorry for myself."

"You were out here crying? I thought you came out to smoke."

"I think I was smoking only to stop myself from crying."

"A lot of the time I was in my bed crying too."

"From now on, Liv, we're going to do a better job letting each other know how we're feeling about things. Deal?" She raised her orange juice glass.

"Deal." Livvie raised her glass too and clinked it against Mom's.

Livvie and Mom spent the rest of the day, and the weekend, mostly hanging out in their apartment. They napped and played cards and read. And talked, a lot, in a way they had never done before. Despite all the good conversation with Mom, though, Livvie's mind was a jumble. Lika. Monsieur Nasri. Albert. Dad. Becky Catrell.

"Why don't you call Dad," Mom suggested on Saturday afternoon. "It might be good to talk with him too."

"We talked last weekend. We usually talk every other week."

"That's okay. You can call him a week early. Besides, we need to make plans for your summer visit."

"All right. I guess I could call him."

Livvie waited until it was 9 a.m. there so Dad could sleep in. He still sounded a little drowsy when he answered the phone. "Hello?"

"Hi, Dad. It's Livvie."

"Livvie? Hi, honey. What's up?"

"I just thought I'd call."

"Well, this is a nice surprise. You know I always love to hear from you. How's school?"

"Fine. School's fine. How's Clover doing?"

"Oh, you know. Up to her usual tricks. Is it hot over there? We're having a late spring. The daffodils are barely out."

"It's been nice here. Pretty warm."

"Lucky you. So, what's up, Livbug?"

After more of the usual conversation about school and Clover and the Red Sox, they decided on the first two weeks in August for her visit. A few times, Livvie heard a woman's voice faintly in the background, a voice she remembered hearing before during other calls. She didn't ask Dad about it though. She would wait for him to tell her about it himself when she saw him in the summer.

On Sunday afternoon Livvie and Mom went for a long bike ride around town. Mom suggested they ride down Cours Mirabeau. Part of Livvie wanted to go see Albert, to introduce him to Mom, to explain everything. But she didn't want to have to tell him about Lika. About how they were friends again, but then how it all got wrecked. So she told Mom that the Cours would be too crowded with all the weekend tourists and she would rather stay on the side streets.

Part of her wanted to call Lika also. To try to talk to her about what happened. To tell her how sorry she was. Again. But Livvie was too afraid. She dreaded Monday when she would have to face her at school. She dreaded what she would see in her eyes. If Lika would even look at her.

Chapter 32

On Sunday night Livvie was about to get into the tub for a good, long soak when the phone rang. Mom answered it and called in that it was for Livvie. She wrapped a towel around herself and went to pick up the phone.

She wasn't sure who it possibly could be since she didn't get many calls, but it turned out to be the last person she expected.

"Allô?" Livvie said.

"Salut, Livvie. It's Lika."

"Lika? Salut!" Livvie almost dropped her towel.

"Ça va?"

"Oui, ça va bien."

"I was worried about you when you weren't in school on Friday."

"Oh, yeah. Mom and I were so wiped out from everything that she thought we needed a day off. How are you?"

"I'm fine."

"How's your Papa?"

"He's fine too. He was just kind of in shock on Thursday night. With everything that happened."

"I'm so sorry about that. My mom is too."

"It's okay. I talked with him and Maman for a long time about it. About a lot of things we've never talked about but needed to. They said they would have done the same thing if I'd been missing. And they said for you to make sure you tell your maman where you are next time."

"I definitely will."

"I'll see you tomorrow?"

"Yes! See you tomorrow!"

Livvie danced back to the bathroom.

The next day at lunch, Nicole waved to Livvie from a table saying, "Olivia, sit here! Were you sick on Friday?" She patted the empty seat beside her. Pilar and Gabrielle sat across from Nicole, and Sylvie sat in the chair beside the empty seat. The rest of the chairs at the table were already taken.

"I'd like to sit with Malika today also," Livvie said, nodding to Lika standing beside her. "But it doesn't look like there's enough room here, so I think we'll go over there." She pointed to an empty table. "Do you all want to come?"

Nicole's eyebrows knitted together to form a dark V on her forehead. Livvie wasn't sure if that meant she was mad or hurt or merely confused. Shaking her head, Nicole said to the other girls, "We'll stay here, oui?"

The girls didn't say anything. Sylvie looked like she was about to, but stopped herself. So Livvie and Lika went over to the other table and sat down. Livvie poured Lika a glass of water, Lika passed Livvie the basket of bread, and they settled into a comfortable conversation. The Chipies kept looking over at them and whispering though. Nicole's eyebrows kept forming that V, and Sylvie kept peering over her shoulder, her ponytail bobbing like a piece of driftwood.

Livvie tried to ignore their looks and focus on Lika, her dark eyes warm and open. But a gulf was forming between the cafeteria tables. As if the floor had given out and left Livvie and Lika stranded on one little island and Nicole, Sylvie, Pilar, and Gabrielle on another. And the water between them was vast and perilous.

Livvie could have been content to stay on the little island with Lika. But something inside her was determined to find a way to cross those waters, with Lika alongside her. For all their pettiness and cliquishness, Livvie did like the Chipies. They were fun to hang out with. And they had been nice to her when she had needed it. She wished they wouldn't act so weird about Lika though. If only they could get over their hang-ups and get to know her, Livvie was sure they would like her. And maybe she would like them too.

At recess, Livvie asked Lika if she wanted to go over with Nicole's group by the wall. But she said, "I don't know. I think I'd rather sit on our bench."

"That's okay. Me too."

When school ended, Livvie invited Lika to go get some glace. As they walked through the courtyard, Livvie linked her arm through Lika's. The Chipies were standing outside the gate chatting like they usually did. Livvie held her other arm out and said, "Nicole, do you and the others want to go get some glace with me and Malika?"

"Um, non, we're doing something else today." There was that V.

Sylvie started to say something, but stopped again. Pilar looked down at her skirt and smoothed it out, and Gabrielle slipped her arm through Nicole's.

Livvie felt like shouting, "What's the big deal? Can't we get over this?" But she said instead, "Okay, see you tomorrow." She would have to come up with a better way to try to bridge the gulf. There had to be a way.

As she turned with Lika to walk toward Cours Mirabeau, Livvie felt Nicole's eyes on her back. But she shook them off. It was a beautiful day, perfect for a stroll down to the Cours. The sky was a clear blue and the window box geraniums were splashing their colors everywhere. Pre-season tourists crowded the streets. Albert had to be there today. Even though neither of them mentioned him specifically, Livvie sensed that Lika was thinking the same thing. And, sure enough, when they got to the top of the Cours, Lika said, "Oh, good. He is there today."

Albert was busy at work. As they approached him, he was in the middle of a pose Livvie had seen him do a few times before. It was a crowd pleaser. He was pretending to be a strongman. His arms were raised up as if to show off his muscles and his cheeks were puffed out. Since he was a small, thin man, the pose was especially funny. The crowd of tourists surrounding him laughed and snapped photos.

When they joined the crowd, Albert's eyes met Livvie's. Then he looked at Lika. At their linked arms. He held his pose a moment longer, released his hands, and shook out his arms. The small crowd applauded and dropped some money in his bowl.

Next, he squatted beside his box and fiddled with the side of it, like he was trying to open it. Livvie had never seen him do this before. "I wonder what he's going to do," she whispered to Lika.

"I don't know. This one's something new."

He opened the pretend door and reached his hands inside. Slowly he drew his hands back as if he was holding something fragile. Something alive. Standing up, he brought it to his heart before raising it up in the air. He held it like that for a few seconds, grasping the creature. It was a bird. Suddenly he released it into the air and stepped back, watching it fly up into the sky. All of the eyes in the crowd followed the bird as it made its way up, into the empty, blue sky. It was a dove, Livvie was certain of it. The dove of peace. When she brought her eyes back down to earth, they met Albert's again. His face bore the slightest hint of a smile.

Lika pulled Livvie a little closer to her and said, "It's beautiful, n'est-ce pas? The dove."

"Yes, it is."

They stood there over an hour, arms linked, watching Albert, the glace completely forgotten. They laughed, and ooohed, and ahhhed, and clapped with the groups of people that came and went. Albert was especially animated, as if he was performing his best for Livvie and Lika.

Finally there was a break in the crowd, and Livvie and Lika were the only ones left standing by him.

"Bonjour, Livvie. And you must be Malika," he said, speaking to them right there on the street.

"Oui. But you can call me Lika. And you're Albert."

"I'm pleased to meet you, Lika." He bowed. "And how are you, Livvie? You had some people worried about you last week, non?"

"Yeah, I'm sorry about that. It's all okay now though."

"I'm glad to hear that. You girls are going to be experts in miming by the end of the day. But I think you both already are. For some people, miming comes naturally. Others need to be taught—or reminded—how to do it, and must work at it."

Just then, three young children ran up to them. They pointed at Albert and shouted to their trailing parents in a language Livvie didn't recognize. Albert immediately got into his strongman pose again and the children were transfixed.

The parents wandered up to join them. Above his puffed silver cheeks, Albert winked at Livvie and Lika. It was time for them to leave anyway, so they waved goodbye and strolled back toward home through the lovely, narrow streets of Aix, their arms still linked.

Chapter 33

That night while Livvie was helping to make dinner, she told Mom about Lika and Albert. How everything was okay and they were all friends again.

"That's great, Livvie. I had a feeling it would work out. That you would find a way." Mom chopped some zucchini into small chunks and scraped the pieces into a bowl. "You know, your birthday's coming up in a couple weeks. Do you want to do something special with Lika?"

"I don't know. I hadn't thought about it." Livvie pushed some sliced onions and garlic around in a sauté pan. With everything that had been going on, Livvie had almost forgotten about her birthday. She would be twelve on May 15th. Back in Vermont, she would have been planning a party with her friends. Like last year, at Lake Iroquois. It had been too cool to swim, but Dad had brought along his kayak and gave everybody lessons. Afterwards, they all had gone back to the house for a cookout.

That all seemed so distant now. Although not in a sad way. It was a good memory, but it was in the past. The safe, comfortable past. The present was harder, but good too. Every day Livvie felt like she learned something about herself and the world. Every day she was making new memories. The onions and garlic sizzled and snapped in the hot oil, filling the small kitchen with their appetizing aroma. Livvie suddenly realized what she wanted to do.

"I want to have a party. Here at the apartment," Livvie said definitively.

"That sounds fun. Who do you want to invite?"

"My friends. Lika. And Nicole and Sylvie and Pilar and Gabrielle."

"Sure. Whoever you want."

"I don't want many presents this year. There's only one thing I want."

"Oh yeah? What's that?"

Livvie told Mom her idea. The one thing she wanted. Mom said she would be delighted to take care of it.

After dinner Livvie got busy making invitations and handed them out the next day at recess. She gave Lika hers first.

"Of course, I'd love to come," Lika said, her eyes shining.

"I'm inviting Nicole and the other girls too. Do you want to come over with me while I hand out the invitations?"

"I don't know… maybe I'll wait here."

"It's okay, Lika. They can be kind of snobby sometimes. But they can be nice too. Once you get to know them. Come over with me."

"Okay," she said, but her eyes had clouded.

As they walked up, the girls were leaning against the wall talking quietly.

"Salut," Livvie said.

All four said "Salut, Olivia" and turned toward them.

Then Sylvie said, "Salut, Malika."

Lika smiled timidly and said, "Salut."

"I'm having a birthday party and I'd love for you all to come," Livvie said, passing out the invitations.

At first, they didn't say anything and all just looked down at the big, American-style birthday cake Livvie had drawn on the cover.

Sylvie opened hers up and broke the silence. "Chouette! Sure, I can come."

"I can too," Pilar said. "It sounds like fun."

Nicole hesitated, her eyes shifting between Sylvie and Pilar. "Me too," she finally said. "I'm with Maman that weekend so I can come."

"Me too," Gabrielle said.

"Great! It'll be the six of us. Plus my Mom. And we're planning a surprise."

"A surprise! What kind of surprise?" Sylvie asked.

"A special surprise. You have to wait and see."

Livvie and Lika stayed over with the Chipies for the rest of recess. Lika was pretty quiet the whole time. Sylvie made an effort to include her, and the other girls were polite. Not exactly warm and friendly, but at least polite. Livvie hoped her party would change things.

Chapter 34

The Saturday morning of Livvie's birthday, she woke up early. Everyone was coming at 11:30, and she and Mom had a lot to do. Monsieur Cantini had agreed to let them have the party in the backyard garden and the weather looked ideal, but the yard needed some cleaning up. The strong mistral that had been blowing the whole week before had left behind fallen branches and scattered debris.

Mom was already up, so after a special breakfast of pancakes and maple syrup, they raked the yard, piling the branches by the back fence. They carried their table and chairs all the way down the stairs, careful not to bump the walls. Livvie hung rainbow-colored streamers and balloons from the trees while Mom set the table. Afterwards she frosted the cake, a big, chocolate layer cake, the kind she made for Livvie every year. She had had to special order the American pans over the Internet.

They were having chicken salad for lunch, Livvie's all-time favorite since she was a little girl. The one time she had ordered chicken salad in France, the first month they had arrived, the waiter had placed a cold chicken breast on a bed of lettuce in front of her. That was their version of chicken salad. At the time, Livvie had thought it was disgusting, but now it was one of her funniest French moments.

Livvie mixed the chicken and mayonnaise up with grapes and walnuts, glad to have a lot to do so the time would pass more quickly. She was excited, like she always was before a birthday party. But this time she was a little nervous too. None of these girls had ever been over to her apartment, and they had only met Mom in passing. Except Lika, of course, who had met Mom during one of her finer moments.

She was also worried about having Lika over with the Chipies. Sylvie had been nice to Lika ever since they had gone over during recess to hand out the invitations. And the other girls had been polite, but it still didn't feel completely comfortable. Sometimes when Livvie and Lika sat with them at lunch, there were long, awkward silences, until Livvie usually said something dumb to break it. Lika wasn't herself around them either.

Livvie hoped being at her apartment, away from school, in a different environment would put everyone more at ease. If that didn't work, maybe the surprise she had planned would. But she was nervous about that too. Even though Mom had assured her it was all arranged, not to worry, it was going to be grand.

Finally, everything was ready around 11:15, so Livvie went into her room to get changed. Mom had picked out a cute new dress for her at Z, one she actually liked. It was made of a silky yellow fabric with big orange flowers dancing across the front. She slipped it on and did a twirl for her stuffed Clover. Her charm bracelet jingled on her wrist. "What do you think, Clover? How do I look?" she said.

As she was putting on a pair of pearl earrings Dad had sent for her birthday, the doorbell rang. To let someone in, you had to go all the way down the stairs to open the main door, so Livvie ran down in her bare feet. The whole time down she was thinking, I hope it's Lika, I hope it's Lika. She opened the door and it was.

Lika was with her mom, who carried a basket full of vegetables from the market. Her emerald green headscarf shimmered in the sunlight.

"Salut, Lika. Bonjour, Madame."

"Salut, Livvie. Bon Anniversaire." Lika kissed Livvie on both cheeks and handed her a small package.

"Bon Anniversaire, Olivia," Madame Nasri said, leaning down to exchange kisses also.

"Merci. Come on in. You're the first ones here. The party's going to be back in the garden, but my mom's still upstairs."

They followed her up to the apartment. As they rounded the corner near the top of the stairs, Mom was waiting in the doorway. "Bonjour, Madame. Bonjour, Malika," Mom said. "We're so glad you're here. Please come in."

Mom extended her hand to Madame Nasri, who took it, saying, "Bonjour, Madame."

"Please, call me Diane."

"Okay, Diane. I'm Karima. Olivia tells me you work for Dell?"

Mom and Madame Nasri started talking about work, so Livvie took Lika into her bedroom.

Lika walked over to the photos on Livvie's dresser. The one of Dad on their front porch. A new one of Annabel, Sarah, and Kendall that they had sent for her birthday. The one of Clover. Lika pointed to that one and said, "Is this your cat?"

"Yeah, that's Clover."

"It looks like the one over there." She pointed to the stuffed cat on Livvie's bed.

"Yeah, that's Clover's stand-in."

"Is this your Papa?"

"Yeah, that's Dad. And these are my friends from back in Vermont."

Lika was about to say something else when the doorbell rang again.

"Livvie, do you want me to answer the door?" Mom called in.

"No, I'll get it." Livvie went back out into the foyer and Lika followed.

"I'll walk down with you, Olivia. I need to get these vegetables home," Madame Nasri said. "It was nice to meet you, Diane."

"It was my pleasure. Let me know next time you're over at Dell. We could meet for lunch."

"I would like that. Have a nice time at the party, Malika."

Lika kissed her mom goodbye and Livvie walked back down the stairs with Madame Nasri. When she opened the front door, Nicole and Gabrielle stood there smiling. But their smiles quickly faded. Their eyes were focused behind Livvie at Madame Nasri. At her headscarf.

"Salut, Nicole, Gabrielle. This is Madame Nasri. Malika's mother." Livvie held her breath.

Their smiles returned, but they were stiff and forced. "Bonjour, Madame," Nicole said, followed by Gabrielle. Like usual.

"Bonjour, Nicole, Gabrielle," she said, nodding at them. "I hope you have a wonderful party, Olivia."

"Merci, Madame. Au revoir." Livvie let her breath out.

Madame Nasri turned to head up the street, and Gabrielle handed Livvie a large package wrapped in fancy purple and gold paper. Livvie thanked her and when she was finished admiring the paper, Nicole held out a card. She looked away as if embarrassed, saying quietly, "I have to get your present later. When I'm with Papa next weekend in Paris. Maman couldn't ….I'm sorry."

"No problem, Nicole. It's okay. I'm just glad you're in Aix this weekend so you could come."

Nicole smiled, more genuinely this time, though her gray eyes looked sad. Livvie led them upstairs and, as they reached the top, the bell rang again. Livvie let Nicole and Gabrielle in and ran back downstairs. She tried to walk quietly past the Durands' entryway thinking they wouldn't be thrilled about all the shoes on the stairs. When she opened the door, it was Sylvie and Pilar, who had a new haircut. Shorter than before, and much curlier now.

"It's for summer," Pilar said. "For the swim team. My long hair was way too hard to manage."

"I like your smiley face," Sylvie said, pointing to the door.

"Yeah, he's cute, isn't he?" Livvie said.

They handed Livvie their presents and followed her upstairs, chattering about Pilar's busy schedule of swim practices. Back in the apartment, Mom was in the kitchen with Lika, Nicole, and Gabrielle. She was charming them with her description of American chicken salad and passing out platters of food to be carried to the garden. She greeted Pilar and Sylvie by handing them bowls of strawberries.

As they all entered the backyard, the table looked picture perfect under the fig and pomegranate trees. Its floral tablecloth fluttered in the warm breeze. Low-growing rosemary and lavender plants lined the fence surrounding the small yard, perfuming the air. In the background, beyond the fence and the parking lot, out beyond the trees and the suburbs of Aix, rose Sainte Victoire, like a giant, silver crown.

Livvie paused, taking it all in. Then people began to enter the picture. First Mom, setting a pitcher of lemonade on the table and smiling over at Livvie. And Lika placing a platter of chicken salad down while asking Mom something about it. Nicole and Gabrielle put down their platters, Nicole still with that sad look in her eyes. Pilar joined the picture, setting down her bowl of berries and brushing back her curls. Finally Sylvie put down her bowl and looked over at Livvie.

"Who's the other person coming, Olivia? There are eight places." Sylvie's words pulled Livvie back into the picture.

"That's the surprise," Livvie said.

They all immediately shouted out guesses.

"Monsieur Simon!"

"Paul!"

"Thomas!"

"One of Pilar's brothers!"

"Your Papa!"

"Madame la Directrice!"

They laughed and called out names. Only Lika stayed quiet, looking at Livvie with a knowing smile on her face.

Suddenly they stopped. Their eyes were fixed behind Livvie, at the gate. She turned around and there was Albert, his silver skin radiant as noon. "Albert!" Livvie cried. "You're here!" She ran over to him and hugged him. Some of his silver paint rubbed off onto her shoulder.

He stepped back and did one of his elaborate bows. When Livvie looked over at the girls, they were staring at him, eyes wide. But Lika was beaming. Mom too.

"Everybody, this is my friend, Albert."

"So you do know him," Sylvie said.

"I do now. I've gotten to know him recently. And I wanted him to come to my party. To teach us all how to mime."

"He's an expert," Lika said, walking over to join them.

Albert put his hand on her arm and nodded hello. A small smudge of luminous silver stayed on her skin.

"I would certainly like to learn," Mom said. "You're never too old to learn something new. How do we start?"

He walked over to the table and reached into the bag he had brought along. As he took out a bouquet of purple flowers, real ones, Livvie remembered the plastic ones he had held out to Mom back in the fall. The ones she had scoffed at. He bowed and handed the bouquet to Mom. "Thank you. How lovely," she said.

But he put his finger to his lips and shook his head.

"Oh, I get it. I'm not supposed to say anything. Oops!" Mom put her hand over her mouth.

He nodded, and Mom stood there for a moment, thinking. Then she put the flowers to her nose and inhaled deeply. Lifting them up in the air, she twirled a few times, her skirt flaring like a Spanish dancer's. She ended with a deep curtsy, almost toppling over in her flat sandals.

Albert was impressed. He applauded and gave her the thumbs up. Mom did another curtsy, but this time she kept her balance. When she stood up, she cradled the flowers. Livvie could tell by the hint of regret on her face that she remembered the incident with the plastic ones too.

Livvie and Lika applauded too, clapping loudly. The others joined in, but with reticence. Mom took a seat and the girls followed. Except for Livvie, who kept standing. Albert turned to her, waving her to his side. He dropped into a crouch and she followed his lead, crouching beside him. He moved slowly forward, still in a crouch, so she did too. Gradually, he moved faster, holding his arms out from his sides and straightening his legs. Livvie followed behind him as he circled the yard, faster and faster, until she was standing upright and running as hard as she cold. He flapped his arms, so Livvie did too. She felt like she was flying, flying around the yard, circling the table and Mom, Lika and the other girls. She felt like she could take off and soar to the top of Sainte Victoire.

Albert gradually slowed down and looked back at Livvie, smiling. Livvie smiled too and they flew along together one more time around the yard. Slowing back down to a walk, they rejoined the others.

"Bravo! Bravo!" Mom cried. Lika cheered and clapped, and the others followed with more gusto this time. Even Nicole. Livvie returned to her seat, but inside she still felt like she was flying.

To Livvie's surprise, Pilar volunteered to go next. Albert motioned her forward and looked at her for a moment with his hand on his chin. Then he slowly moved his hands up and down as if he was playing the drums. Softly at first. Pilar imitated him, pretending to sit behind a big set of drums. They picked up the pace, playing harder, and before long Pilar was banging away at the drums and a cymbal too. Albert stopped to watch her as she kept on going, her black curls flying wildly around her face. Everybody cheered and clapped and laughed. Pilar kept on jamming until she was laughing too, until finally she looked like she might collapse from exhaustion. Albert shook his head as if amazed, and gave her a big salute.

"We need to sign you up with the Rolling Stones!" Mom said.

While Pilar stumbled toward a chair to catch her breath, Albert looked the group over. He pointed at Gabrielle, who covered her eyes with her hands and peeked through her fingers. Albert kept pointing until she reluctantly walked up to the front. He put his hands on his hips and frowned, scratching his chin. Then he shook out his arms. Gabrielle laughed nervously and did the same. He shook his arms harder, so Gabrielle did too. Bending his knees, Albert reached straight down with both of his arms. He grasped something and looked forward clenching his teeth. Instantly Livvie recognized his strongman act. He was reaching down for his barbell. The last thing

Livvie could imagine was graceful, elegant Gabrielle as a strongman. But she followed his lead. After all, she had had a lot of practice following Nicole.

Gabrielle grasped and grimaced. She strained to raise the barbell in front of her chest, puffing out her cheeks like Albert. Gritting her teeth, she squeezed her eyes shut as she pressed the barbell above her head. Everyone applauded, Albert too. She stood there for several more seconds with her eyes still shut, reveling in the moment. Finally she dropped the barbell and strutted around triumphantly, showing off her muscles, which somehow did look surprisingly impressive in her pale pink sundress.

They all laughed and clapped and cheered, "Hurray for Gabrielle! Gabrielle the strongwoman!"

Albert patted her on the back and she glowed.

It was Sylvie's turn next. Albert waved her to the front and she made a muscle too. But Albert shook his head. He had another idea for her. He reached down to pick something up and began digging with an imaginary shovel. He was digging a hole. He gestured for her to do the same, so she picked up an imaginary shovel and started digging a hole also. They kept digging until their holes were deep enough, then put down their shovels. Albert walked a few steps away and Sylvie followed. He leaned down to pick up something else, something cumbersome. Sylvie did the same, struggling under its weight. They carried these things over to their holes and gently placed them in. Albert straightened his, and finally Livvie got it. They were planting something. A tree or shrub of some sort? They scooped the dirt in, and Albert stepped back while Sylvie continued on her own. Patting the dirt down, mulching the plant, and finally watering it. She glanced over at Albert and watered his plant too.

Albert nodded in approval, and Sylvie nodded too. Livvie realized she was nodding along with them, at what they had planted there in the arid dirt of the backyard, under the brilliant Mediterranean sun. For some reason, it made her think back to when she and Mom had first arrived in Aix. Back to that taxi ride from the TGV station. When Livvie had looked around and all she saw was brown and brittle and parched. She didn't see the wild rosemary and lavender, the olive trees and umbrella pines. She didn't appreciate how they thrived in the rugged beauty of this landscape. Livvie realized she didn't see and appreciate so much her first few months in France. But now, almost a year later, she felt certain, and grateful, that whatever it was Albert and Sylvie had planted would grow. Not only grow, but flourish.

Livvie clapped along with everyone else, and laughed when Albert picked up the pretend watering can and splashed water on Sylvie. She hammed it up and took cover behind her chair. As the applause died down, Lika and Nicole both said at the same time, "I'll go next."

Albert waved the two of them forward. They both hesitated, but got up from their chairs and joined him. He positioned them so they were facing each other, about ten feet apart. Walking between them, he paced out a big square. Outside the square, he reached down to the ground and lifted up something heavy and rounded, like a large stone. Straining under its weight, he carried it to the outside edge of the square and placed it on the ground. Then he did it again, placing the next stone beside the first. He motioned to Lika and Nicole to join him.

Reaching down, they each picked up a heavy stone. They struggled to carry the stones to the edge of the square and laid them side by side. Albert nodded and motioned for them to continue while he stepped out of the way. So they did it again, and again, and again, until they had covered the outline of the square with stones. They looked over at Albert, not sure what to do next.

He gestured that they needed to place another layer of stones on top of the first. They looked at each other and raised their eyebrows, but kept going. They lifted and carried and placed stones, positioning them beside each other's. Until at some point, they both seemed to understand what it was they were creating. Four walls enclosing a space. A building of some sort. A home? A school?

As everyone sat there watching Lika and Nicole work together, intent on their task, something happened. It was almost like magic. Livvie felt it and she was certain everyone else did too. Especially Lika and Nicole. So by the time they were done—and somehow they both knew when that was—by the time they stepped back, on the same side now, admiring what they had built, they had been changed in some way.

Everyone had been quiet the whole time they were working. So quiet that the air seemed to vibrate. But when they finished, everyone burst into applause. Nicole grabbed Lika's hand, and the silver smudge on Lika's arm glinted in the sun. There was one on Nicole's elbow now too, and it winked as they bowed.

Livvie looked over at Albert and he was clapping too, not loudly, but with meaning. Like all of his gestures had. But he looked less like a mime at that moment than a teacher. A teacher who was pleased with his students' work.

Lika and Nicole dropped hands and went back to their chairs, the magic still there between them.

Chapter 35

Applause rang out from above. It was the Durands, standing on their balcony surrounded by several carefully clipped topiary plants. Livvie didn't know how long they'd been standing there watching, but she called up to them. "It's my birthday! Come celebrate with us!"

They looked at each other and, to Livvie's astonishment, they nodded and turned to go downstairs.

Mom announced that they needed to invite Monsieur Cantini too, so she knocked on his back door. Within minutes, the two of them were coming out of his apartment carrying three more chairs. Livvie introduced everyone as they squeezed the extra chairs around the table. When Albert shook hands with the Durands and Monsieur Cantini, he left little smudges of silver on their skin too. There wasn't anyone at the party whose skin was left untouched by his silver paint.

Sitting between Sylvie and Lika, Livvie gazed around at all the faces at the table. The faces of her friends and family in Aix. Mom at the head of the table and Albert at the other end. Nicole on the other side of Lika. Pilar and Gabrielle. The Durands. Monsieur Cantini. It didn't seem possible that, at her last birthday, with the exception of Mom she didn't know any of them. And now she felt a closeness, a deep connectedness, with some of them that she had never felt in Vermont. Especially to Lika. And to Mom too.

Mom passed around the platters of food above everyone's lively chatter. Everyone but Albert, of course. Just when Livvie was wondering if he was going to stay silent during the entire meal, Madame Durand asked him how he got into miming. He came right out and answered her, and the whole table stopped talking. He broke the silence by making a joke about a mime who was a TV reporter and soon the conversation picked up again, harmonized by Albert's rich, warm voice.

When Mom went to get the cake, Monsieur Cantini disappeared inside his apartment. As she carried the cake over to the table, he reappeared with his violin and played "Happy Birthday" for Livvie. The music floated in the air, catching in the branches of the fig and pomegranate trees before drifting up into the sky. Everyone tried their best to sing in English, and it was the most beautiful version of "Happy Birthday" Livvie had ever heard. Mom placed the cake in front of Livvie, and the flames of its twelve candles shined like miniature suns.

"Make a wish quick, before they go out," Mom said.

But Livvie's wish had already come true, so she wished for her wish to keep on coming true, forever. She blew out the candles and everyone cheered, Albert the loudest. Then she cut the cake while Mom passed slices around. It had never tasted better.

When it was time to open presents, they all helped clear the table and carry them over. Livvie didn't want to open the gifts in any particular order, so she reached out and grabbed one without looking. It was Lika's. She had made a beautiful card with a pastel drawing of the two of them sitting on their bench. The background was a lush, dream-like green. Inside it said, "I'm glad we're friends."

"Merci, Lika. I am too," Livvie said, her eyes stinging.

She unwrapped the small package to find a ceramic tile, painted in bright colors. It was inscribed with the words, "Un vrai ami est le plus grand trésor." A true friend is the greatest treasure. Livvie read it out loud and the words caught in her throat.

"It's beautiful. I'll hang it in my room. Above my bookcase," Livvie said, staring at the tile's swirling vines and flowers surrounding words that a year ago would have made no sense to her. She would have understood neither the language, nor the depth of meaning in the words.

"Do mine next, Livvie!" Pilar called out, pushing her present towards Livvie.

Mom took the tile, admiring its design, while Livvie unwrapped Pilar's gift. It was a red and white striped beach bag with a matching towel. "For when you come to my pool this summer," Pilar said.

"I love it, Pilar! Merci, I can't wait to come."

"You all can come," Pilar said, looking around the circle. Her eyes lingered on Lika.

The next present was Gabrielle's. When Livvie pulled the wrapping off, she instantly recognized it. It was a large, white linen pillow, like the one she had given Nicole for her birthday. "Olivia" was embroidered in the same ornate, pink script.

"It's gorgeous, Gabrielle. Merci."

"My grand-mère makes them and sells them. She's teaching me how, so I helped her with that one."

"It's beautiful. Does your maman make them too?"

"Non, she's not interested in sewing. But I'm glad Grand-mère's teaching me."

Sweet, strongwoman Gabrielle. Livvie was finally starting to see a little of the real person inside.

Two presents were left, and Nicole's envelope. Livvie picked up the envelope while Nicole explained to everyone that she wanted to wait to get Livvie something fabulously chic in Paris the next weekend. Livvie played along, gushing about the card and how much she loved Paris. But a shadow still darkened Nicole's eyes.

Livvie recognized Sylvie's present so she chose it next, thinking the last one on the table was from Mom.

Her card was thicker than usual and, when Livvie opened it, a train ticket fell out. "It's to Cassis," Sylvie said. "To come visit me this summer."

"I'd love to! Can I go, Mom? Please?"

"I think that's a fine idea," Mom said.

"Merci!" Livvie cried to both of them.

In the little box that came with the card was a silver charm. It was a tiny replica of "Old Mossy," Livvie's favorite fountain on Cours Mirabeau.

"I almost got you something from Z," Sylvie said. "But I thought you might like this better. For your charm bracelet."

"It's perfect, Sylvie." Livvie held it up to her bracelet, next to the Eiffel Tower. And Grandma's heart.

The last present was wrapped in modest white tissue paper. There was no card. Livvie picked it up, saying to Mom, "It's from you, right?"

"Non." Mom shook her head and looked puzzled.

Nobody in the group spoke up. As soon as Livvie unwrapped it, though, she knew who it was from. The paper fell away and she was holding a small tube of silver paint in her hand. "But you already gave me a gift, Albert," Livvie said.

"Non, Livvie, I didn't give that to you. You gave it to yourself."

After everyone had left and Livvie and Mom had cleaned up the backyard, they took the leftover cake into the living room. They put their feet up on the coffee table and leaned back into the deep couch.

"I can't believe how wrong I was about Albert," Mom said, balancing the cake platter on their laps and taking a big spoonful.

"I'm not gonna say 'I told you so.'" Livvie took a spoonful too, with extra frosting.

"Well, you deserve to. He's such a nice man. You know, he wouldn't even let me pay him for coming to perform. He said he was there as a guest, not a performer. So I suppose that means I owe you a birthday present."

"No, it's okay. I got exactly what I was hoping for."

"I'm glad. And I can't believe his son lives in Phoenix! Did you know that?"

"No way! I just knew his son lived in the US."

"He and Grandma are practically neighbors. What a small world it is.

You know, I was trying to figure out all afternoon who Albert reminds me of and I think I finally have. Grandpa. He reminds me of Grandpa."

"Yeah, he does."

"Next time Grandma comes, she has to meet him."

Livvie licked the rich frosting off her spoon, thinking about how small a world it really was. She set her spoon down on the table, feeling full, content. Or at least almost. There was only one thing missing. One more piece to fill in the picture. As if on cue, the phone started to ring.

It was Dad. As soon as Livvie answered the phone, he began singing "Happy Birthday," hamming it up with sound effects. He did a Rhythm and Blues version, his voice straining on the high notes.

"Thanks, Dad," Livvie said, laughing. "And for the earrings too."

"You're welcome, Livbug. But your big present is waiting for you here. I couldn't send it, so you can bring it back with you when you visit this summer."

"What is it?"

"You have to guess."

"A new bike?"

"No."

"Skis?"

"Nope."

"A skateboard?"

"No, you're way off. Here's a hint."

Livvie waited, listening. At first she didn't hear anything except, faintly in the background, that female voice again. It bothered her but, for some reason, not as much as it had before. Then she heard a soft humming sound. Clover's purr. "Clover? Is it Clover?"

"You guessed it! I'm making arrangements for you to bring him back to France with you. He misses you way too much."

"Oh, Daddy! Thank you!"

Another unexpected gift, and just the right one. Finally, at long last, she was feeling full.

Chapter 36

Two months later

Their feet kicked up small clouds of dust. Pebbles scattered and their sneakers slipped a little as they made their way up the gentle slope. Livvie had expected it to be steeper, more difficult. If it wasn't for the blazing July sun shining down on them, this would almost have been a leisurely climb.

"Look, Lika! A scorpion!" Livvie cried. "Wow, I've never seen one before." The tiny creature was much more delicate than she had imagined. As they stepped closer, it scurried under a large rock.

"Chouette! This looks like a good place for us to rest too," Lika said, walking over to another rock and sitting down. She pulled out her water bottle, took a drink, and offered it to Livvie.

"Merci. How far back do you think they are?"

"Not sure. Maybe we should wait for them to catch up."

"You think we're about halfway?"

"Yeah, that's what I would guess."

A few minutes later they heard voices in the distance, Mom's and Madame Nasri's. The voices got closer and before long the moms were winding up the chalky path toward Livvie and Lika.

"There you are! Karima and I were wondering if we wouldn't see you again until the top," Mom said, breathing hard.

"A water break, good idea!" Madame Nasri said. Her face gleamed under her cotton headscarf.

Livvie held the bottle out to Madame Nasri. She took a long drink and passed it to Mom.

Climbing Sainte Victoire had been Livvie's idea. She had been thinking about it for a while and, when she mentioned it to Lika, she immediately wanted to come along. They thought it would be fun for both of their moms to go too, making it a mother/daughter adventure. Mom had never been big on hiking, so Livvie was surprised when she had been enthusiastic about it. Lika said her mom had been too, which had shocked her because of her mom's fear of heights.

But both moms had gotten into the whole idea. They had put together an elaborate picnic lunch, which they took turns carrying in a backpack. Madame Nasri had even bought a new pair of hiking shoes. They had laughed and joked at the trailhead about who was going to carry the other one back down the mountain. But once they started out, they got involved in a conversation and didn't seem to mind the hiking.

Mom passed the bottle back to Lika, who took another drink and handed it again to Livvie. They continued passing it around in a circle until it was empty.

Looking up the path toward the top, Livvie said, "C'mon. Let's keep going. We're halfway there."

"You girls go on ahead if you want. Don't wait for us," Mom said, taking off her baseball cap and wiping her forehead. Her hair had gotten longer and was pulled back in a ponytail. It was lighter too because she hadn't been coloring it lately.

"Okay, we'll meet you at the top," Lika said, standing.

Livvie and Lika continued up, following the path winding through the flowering rosemary, the pine and oak trees. Livvie hadn't expected trees on the trail. From the view of Sainte Victoire from their apartment, it had looked like a massive hunk of silver rock with jagged peaks. But like so many other things Livvie had discovered that year, when she allowed herself to get in close, when she made the effort to get to know something, or someone, better, things were often very different from how they appeared.

The path got steeper as they climbed, but they kept on going. Sometimes they were quiet, the only sound their feet crunching on the white pebbles. Sometimes they talked. Mostly about friends from school and what they had all been up to since the school year had ended. During the final weeks of the semester, they had sat with Sylvie, Pilar, Gabrielle, and Nicole every day at lunch and had hung out with them at recess. There were none of those awkward silences anymore. Instead, there was a lot more laughter. Sure, Nicole could still be a pain sometimes, especially when she acted all snooty. But Livvie tried to ignore it. And Lika seemed to also.

Ever since Livvie's party, they all seemed more comfortable just being themselves. It was as if that magic silver paint Albert had touched everyone with had stayed on their skin. Or maybe, the magic had worked its way in, underneath their skin. It had touched all of them deep inside, where it mattered.

Like the weekend before, when Pilar had invited the five of them over to her pool. Livvie had finally gotten to meet her infamous twin brothers. But Livvie was more excited about all of them being together again. Nicole had even come down for a few days from Paris where she was spending the summer with her father. They had all floated around on inflatable lounges drinking lemonade, talking, and laughing. Lika had laughed the hardest, especially when Pilar's dog jumped in the pool and swam around between everyone. Livvie had even told them about her old nickname for them, the Chipies, and they all got a kick out of that.

At one point Sylvie had asked Lika a question about Islam, and that got a whole conversation going about religion. They must have talked about it for at least an hour. Everyone was curious about Muslim traditions and holidays, about the headscarf and what went on at a mosque. Lika had explained about her customs and beliefs and asked the rest of them questions about theirs. During the conversation, Livvie found out Gabrielle was Jewish, so she learned some new things about that religion too.

Livvie had seen Lika a few other times since school had gotten out. One Friday, Lika's family had taken Livvie to Marseille with them. She had met some of Lika's relatives, and they had ridden on the big, old-fashioned carousel on la Canebière with her little cousins. Livvie even had gotten to visit her mosque. It was so beautiful and tranquil inside. The walls were decorated with colorful mosaics made up of thousands of tiny pieces of tile. Together, the tiny pieces formed elaborate patterns and images. Afterwards, they had sipped sweet mint tea and eaten pastries at the café next door while traditional North African musicians performed. In the café gift shop Livvie had bought a small pottery bowl painted in the same colors that were on the plates at Lika's house. She kept it on her desk and it held coins. And the tube of silver paint.

As for Albert, Livvie had seen him several times since her party. After all, she always knew where to find him. Once, when she was with Mom and he was finishing up for the day, he had invited them back to his apartment. They had met his wife, Yvette, and he had shown them photos of his son Luc back in Phoenix. Luc's wife was expecting a baby and Albert was ecstatic about being a grandfather. Mom said next time they visited Grandma they were going to look Luc and his family up.

Livvie's trip back to the states was coming up in a few weeks. She and Mom would be in Vermont for a week, then she would go down and stay the rest of the time with Dad. She was looking forward to seeing everyone—Annabel, Sarah, Kendall, and especially Dad. Even though she knew certain parts of the visit would be hard. Like the Becky Catrell part. But she also knew she would be okay. That she was strong enough to face anything.

Mom said it would probably feel weird to be back in the US, that certain things that used to be so familiar there would look strange. Like yellow school buses, or street signs. And that everything would look bigger, oversized. She said Livvie would quickly readjust though, because where you come from always stays in your blood. Livvie knew she would always be American, no matter where she lived. It was part of who she was. And having those American qualities Albert had described—openness, imagination, bravery, heart—had most likely played a role in how she had adapted to living in France. But she also knew she would be ready to return to Aix at the end of her visit. In the fall she would be starting middle school—they called it collège in France—with all her friends, and she had a feeling it was going to be a great year.

"We're almost there!" Lika cried, pulling Livvie out of her thoughts. As they wound their way around a bend, breathing hard against gravity, the sky opened up. "There's the top!"

"We did it!" Livvie threw her arm around Lika's shoulders.

They made the final push to the summit, where the mountain flattened out into a crest of white rock. White rock against blue sky. The sun beamed down and, sure enough, even from up there, Sainte Victoire shined like silver.

A little chapel from the 1600s was perched at the top. Some other hikers wandered in and out of it. Just beyond the chapel stood the cross, towering about fifty feet high. When Livvie craned her neck to look at it, she thought about the people who had labored up the mountain to build the chapel, to raise the cross. How it was so important to those people to achieve that. And how it was still important to some people to have the cross up there. But how did that make Lika feel, this giant symbol of a religion that wasn't her own reigning down from the highest point in a landscape that was her own? That was Lika's challenge, but she seemed to be finding her way just fine.

"It's amazing up here, isn't it?" Lika held her arms up and took a deep breath. "The view is incredible!"

They looked out over the vast valley. Over fields of lavender, finally in bloom, creating a vivid patchwork of purple and green farmland. Then toward the low-lying mountains leading to Aix and farther beyond to Marseille.

"Regarde! There's the Mediterranean!" Livvie cried. "And on the other side of that lies Algeria."

They squinted into the haze toward the sparkling waters of the sea.

"I guess that means America is over there!" Lika pointed to the right.

"And the North Pole is up there!" Livvie cried.

They spun around, laughing, to see their moms straggling up the path, clutching each other's arms. Mom looked exhausted and Madame Nasri glanced around nervously, but they were both smiling.

"You made it!" Livvie cried.

"Barely," Mom gasped. "I need to get in shape."

"It's really high up here," Madame Nasri said.

"Isn't it amazing, Maman?" Lika ran over to her and grabbed her other arm. "You can see all the way to the Mediterranean!"

Madame Nasri turned and gazed out toward the sea, toward Algeria. Her eyes softened. Her face relaxed.

"I think it's time for lunch," Mom said. "I'm starving!"

Searching for a good place to eat, they wove around the other people at the top, people with binoculars and cameras, maps and sunhats. They spoke in lots of different languages, most of which Livvie didn't recognize. But even though they didn't speak the same language, they all pointed and gazed and shielded their eyes from the sun for a better view. They all held their children's hands and put their arms around their loved ones. That was a language Livvie did recognize, thanks to Albert—a universal language.

Finally they picked a spot overlooking the valley. Not too close to the edge, though, for Madame Nasri's sake. The moms unpacked the picnic while Livvie and Lika looked out at the view, trying to identify familiar sites. As Livvie gazed down at the roads and farms and villages, she thought about how the valley had evolved. How, way, way back, dinosaurs used to live there. Then it was home to that long parade of different cultures, and how each of those cultures had left its mark in some way. The Celtic-Ligurians, the Romans, the Teutons and Ambrons, the Christians, the Visigoths, the Lombards and the Maures, the Counts of Barcelona and the French monarchy—all those cultures that were a part of France's history, and that Livvie had thought didn't have anything to do with her life. But they did. Because she was part of that history now, and Lika too. And Lika's family. And all the other more recent immigrants from Algeria, and from other countries in North Africa and the rest of the world. This valley, this country, was still evolving, as new people, like Livvie, arrived and called it their home.

Mom handed Livvie a plate overflowing food—French cheeses and sliced baguette, Algerian couscous and vegetables, American chicken salad. Together, the foods formed a mosaic, a colorful, delicious whole. Livvie and

Lika leaned against each other, and Livvie realized that, just as places evolve, so do people. That we're all shaped and changed by our experiences. We're all touched by the people we meet and love. And even though we might try to resist it, and it sometimes can be scary and really difficult, change and growth are often one and the same. And, ultimately, we might turn out much better than we ever thought was possible.

Glossary of Foreign Words

(French unless otherwise indicated)

À bientôt!: See you soon!

Aix-en-Provence: name of a small city in southern France

allô: hello

alors: well

Arc de Triomphe: name of a triumphal arch in Paris

Arles: name of a small city in southern France famous for its Roman ruins

Arrêtez!: Stop!

au revoir: goodbye

aussi: also

baguette: long, thin loaf of bread

barbe à Papa: cotton candy (Papa's beard)

beaucoup: a lot

bien: good; well

bises: kisses

bon: good

Bon Anniversaire!: Happy Birthday!

bonjour: hello; good day

bonsoir: goodnight

boulangerie: bakery

boules: game played outdoors with metal balls

café: informal restaurant

café au lait: coffee with milk

calissons: candy made with almond paste

Cassis: name of a small village on the Mediterranean

Cathédrale: cathedral

Ca va?: How's it going?

Ca va bien: Things are going well.

chalets: small, wooden cottage

Champs-Elysées: name of a grand avenue in Paris

Chanukah: Jewish holiday also known as the Festival of Lights (Hebrew)

charmante: charming

chèrie: dear

cheval: horse

cheveux: hair

chic: stylish

chocolat chaud: hot chocolate ·

chouette: cute; neat

collège: middle school

Conciergerie: Medieval palace located in Paris

cours: avenue

Cours Mirabeau: name of a busy, main street in Aix

crèches: manger scenes

crêperie: restaurant that serves crêpes

crêpes: thin pancakes

croissant: crescent roll

d'accord: okay

de: of ; from

deux: two

directrice: principal

Eid-ul-Fitr: an Islamic holiday that falls at the end of Ramadan (Arabic)

et: and

Excusez-nous: Excuse us.

fille: girl; daughter

français: French

glace: ice cream

grand-mère: grandmother

grand-père: grandfather

hijab: headscarf worn by Muslim women (Arabic)

Île St-Louis: name of a small island in the Seine in Paris

Jardin du Luxembourg: Luxembourg Gardens, a large park in Paris

Jean Jaurès: name of a French political leader

je suis: I am

Je t'aime: I love you.

jolie: pretty

Joyeux Noël!: Merry Christmas!

la: the

la Canebière: name of a busy, main street in Marseille

laïcité: secularism

La Rotonde: name of a restaurant in Aix whose name means The Rotunda

Le Bastide: name of a popular café on Cours Mirabeau whose name means The Country House

Le Petit Prince: *The Little Prince*, a classic French novel by Antoine de Saint-Exupéry

Les Deux Garçons: name of a café on Cours Mirabeau whose name means The Two Waiters

Louvre: name of an enormous museum of art and antiquities in Paris (formerly a royal palace)

Luberon: name of picturesque, exclusive area in Provence

ma: my

Madame: Mrs; Madam

Mademoiselle: Miss

Maman: Mom

marché: market

Marseille: name of a large French city situated on the Mediterranean

merci: thank you

Mesdames: plural of Madame

Mesdemoiselles: plural of Mademoiselle

métro: subway

mistral: severe wind

Monoprix: name of a large French department/grocery store

Monsieur: Mr.; Sir

N'est-ce pas?: Isn't that so?

non: no

Notre Dame: name of a famous cathedral in Paris (Our Lady)

nougat: candy made from honey and almonds

Oh là là!: Oh my!

oui: yes

pain au chocolat: butter pastry with chocolate inside

Papa: Dad

Père Noël: Father Christmas; Santa Claus

Place des Prêcheurs: name of a large square in Aix (Preachers' Square)

pour: for

présent: present

Provence: name of a region in southern France

Provençal: from/of Provence

Ramadan: The ninth month of the year in the Islamic calendar that is devoted to fasting (Arabic)

Regarde!: Look!

rez-de-chaussée: ground floor

Rodin: last name of Auguste Rodin, a French sculptor

Sainte Victoire: name of a large mountain in Provence (Holy Victory)

salut: hi

santons: clay figurines displayed at Christmastime

Seine: name of the river that runs through Paris

shukran: thank you (Arabic)

s'il vous plaît: please

Sorbonne: name of a university in Paris

stylo: pen

tante: aunt

tant pis: too bad

tapenade: olive paste

Thermes Sextius: thermal baths named after the Roman General Sextius

Toussaint: French Catholic holiday honoring saints

tout le monde: everyone

très: very

Tu es l'américaine: You are the American.

un: a, one

une grande chemise: a big shirt

Un vrai ami est le plus grand trésor: A true friend is the greatest treasure.

viens: come

Voilà!: Here it is!

vraiment: really

CPSIA information can be obtained at www.ICGtesting.com
Printed in the USA
BVOW02s0245200615

404770BV00004B/11/P